SINGLE DAD BURNING UP

CATHRYN FOX

COPYRIGHT

Single Dad Burning Up

ISBN Ebook: 978-1-989374-22-1
ISBN Print: 978-1-989374-21-4

CALLAN

"Daddy, I'm going to miss Chester."

I glance at my daughter, her mess of blonde hair bouncing as she skips down the near empty hallway beside me. Her bright sequined backpack is weighed down with a year's worth of artwork and the Chester she's referring to is the class pet, a cute guinea pig with white and butterscotch fur. With summer vacation now upon us—Kaitlyn's last day of kindergarten behind her—Chester will be going home with the teacher until the school years starts back up in the fall.

"I'm sure he's going to miss you too," I say, and ruffle her hair as the last of the kids rush from the school to enjoy their summer vacation. Luckily, I have the next few days off from the fire station and I was able to pick Kaitlyn up myself.

She pouts up at me, and my heart squeezes in my too-tight chest. She's been without a mother and baby brother for two years now, and every fucking morning, right after I peel my eyes open, I pray to God I can do right by her.

"Can we get a guinea pig?" she asks.

I swallow against the rawness in my tight throat, and grin

at my little girl. I have such a hard time saying no to her, especially when she blinks up at me with those big blue eyes —her late mother's eyes.

"Please, Daddy."

I scrub my face, and remember the goldfish fiasco. Who knew overfeeding a goldfish would create ammonia in the bowl? I'm a firefighter, not a damn fish keeper. But, yeah, I should have Googled it. Kaitlyn shed a lot of tears in the makeshift funeral in our backyard, and I'd hate for her to go through that again. Then again, every child should have a pet, right? A guinea pig would be less work than a dog.

"We'll see, okay?" I say.

"Yay," she squeals and claps her hands. I can't help but smile. At six years old, she's smart enough to know 'we'll see' really means yes. My little girl has me wrapped around her pinky finger. I'm just glad I found the nail polish remover last night, after she painted said finger neon pink. The guys at the station would have gotten a kick out of that. They're all good guys though, even if they love to goad me. There isn't a single colleague that wouldn't jump to lend a helping hand, and she gets lots of motherly attention from her aunt Melissa—my late wife Zoe's younger sister—and both sets of grandparents, who dote on her.

I arch one brow. "You promise you'll take care of him?"

She gives me an enthusiastic nod, and I just shake my head as we round the corner. "I'm going to call him Gilbert."

"Why Gilbert?" I ask.

Her mouth drops open, like I might be dense. She's probably right. Just when I think I'm nailing this single parenting thing, she grows and changes, presenting different challenges and a hundred more Google searches. Can't wait for her teen years—said no dad ever.

"Because it's cute," she says.

I laugh, but it dies an abrupt death when I take the

hallway corner and smack straight into something...or rather someone. A squeal of surprise wraps around me as books and papers and pens scatter to the floor at my feet. I reach out to steady the woman I nearly knocked on her ass.

"Whoa, are you okay?" I ask, instantly realizing I'd plowed right into Gemma Davis, an old friend from high school. She teaches seventh grade, so we rarely cross paths in the school, but I've always liked her. Zoe took Gemma under her wing when Gemma moved here in high school.

"I'm okay," Gemma says and lifts her head. A wide smile splits her lips when she sees it's me. "Callan. Hi. It's so good to see you, or rather, bump into you."

I sink down and begin to gather up her books. "Sorry, I wasn't paying attention."

Her gaze goes from me to my daughter. "How are you, Kaitlyn?" she asks as she crouches with me to clean up the mess.

"I'm getting a guinea pig," Kaitlyn sings out.

I groan, and cut Gemma a glance. "Lucky me, huh?"

Gemma grins at me. "Don't worry. You're not alone. I think every child in Mrs. Anderson's class wants a guinea pig now. Chester *is* awfully cute." She gives a roll of her shoulder. "I guess it could be worse. The class pet could have been a snake."

I eye her. "Don't tell me—"

"Not me," she says with a quick shake of her head that loosens a tendril of honey-blonde hair from the small clip straining to hold it all together. "Mr. Baily has one." She holds her hands up palms out. "Just preparing you for first grade."

I exhale, my shoulders slumping. "Maybe I shouldn't have given in so easily to the guinea pig." She chuckles as we finish gathering up her music sheets. "I hope I didn't mess everything up."

"It's fine," she says. "I've always wanted to hear Beethoven played out of order."

I cringe. "I'm—"

She puts her hand on my arm. "I'm kidding," she says, and when she realizes she has her hand on me, she pulls it back and clutches the papers tighter. "It's not a big deal. I have lots of time to get them in order, before my summer lessons start."

I swallow and work to ignore the sensations trickling through me. Christ, she barely touched me; it shouldn't be triggering any kind of reaction, especially around the vicinity of my crotch. Jesus, I haven't been with a woman since Zoe, and have no desire to be with anyone. I might not have seen Gemma in a while, but we go way back. No way should a simple touch from her spark something deep inside me. Awaken something that has lain dormant for a very long time now.

"Sounds like an exciting weekend," I tease. But who am I to talk? I can't remember the last time I've been to Burgers and Brews Pub with the guys. Maybe that's why my traitorous cock jumped to the occasion. The guys at the station are always trying to set me up—especially my best friend Mason and his wife Lisa. When Zoe was alive, we always hung out as couples, and our children played. Maybe I ought to take them up on it. Any girl I hook up with would have to know up front that a quick roll in the hay is all I'm looking for, though. I have no more to give.

"I'd prefer a weekend with my music sheets to your dangerous job any day, Callan," she says, her eyes wide. "Running into burning buildings." A quake goes through her. "No thank you."

"It's not so bad," I say and turn to look at Kaitlyn. She's spinning in circles, her arms wide, as she chants *Gilbert* over and over. For a child who's been through a lot, she's always happy and that brings a smile to my face. I must be doing something right. I turn back to Gemma, find her staring at me. The last time we talked she'd just taken the job at the school and was dating a police officer. I remember him being quite a bit older than her.

"How've you been?" I ask. "Are you still with...Ah..." Shit what was his name?

"Brad. No, we broke up. A few months ago."

She averts her gaze, her lids fluttering rapidly as her body tenses. Okay, I'm not an expert on reading body language or anything, but I've clearly hit a sore spot here. Did the guy break her heart or something?

"Oh, someone new?" I ask.

"Nope. No desire. I've decided single is the way to go." I frown at that—but who am I to talk? She plasters on a big smile and turns back to me. "But I'm great. Two months off school to bask in the summer sun. Though I will be helping out at the Boys and Girls club, and a few nights a week, I'll be giving private piano lessons."

"I want to play piano, Daddy," Kaitlyn says. "Can Miss Davis teach me?"

It's not the first time she's asked. Her mom played and always filled our house with music. "We'll—" I stop myself before spouting out my favorite response and getting Kaitlyn's hopes up. I don't even know if Gemma has room in her schedule. "How about we talk about it later?" I say.

Gemma gives me a wink, like she's fully aware of my dilemma with my daughter, and my inability to say no. "She almost had you there, didn't she?"

I chuckle. "I've got to get better at saying no."

"You're doing a fine job with her." She casts a look Kaitlyn's way, a look of longing in her eyes as a small smile touches her naked lips. For a second I wonder if her break-up with Brad had something to do with wanting kids. Obviously, she longs to be a mother. "She's a sweet little girl. Very kind and sincere. Like you."

"Shh," I say and glance around. "I've got a reputation to protect here."

Her lips quirk at the corner, then her smile falls. "You good, Callan?" she asks, her voice soft, and I get what she's asking, what people are still asking two years later.

"I'm good," I lie. I'm as good as can be expected, I guess. Truthfully is anyone ever 'good' again after losing their wife and unborn baby boy? I was once told that when you lose someone you have bad days and days that aren't as bad. I hate that I fully understand that now.

"Do you keep in contact with any of the old gang? Are you and Mason still friends? Wait, he's a firefighter too, right?"

"Yup, still best friends," I say. "Come on, I'll walk you out."

"Sure."

We head toward the doors, and the warm afternoon sun shines down on us, but it does little to loosen the tightness in my lungs. On those bad days, I walk around with an invisible band around my chest, squeezing tight. Who am I kidding? On those days that aren't as bad, the belt is still there. I'm not sure it will ever slacken, and maybe I don't want it to. Maybe I deserve the grief.

Gemma leans into me, her warmth and citrusy scent stirring the controlled storm in my body. Her voice is low, for my ears only when she whispers, "If she's serious about lessons, I do have an opening."

I nod, and consider it. "She would probably love it. Her mom..." I let my words fall off.

"I know," Gemma says, and glances at her feet. "We can talk about it more later if you want."

Her reaction isn't unusual. Most people avoid the subject

of my wife. They don't know whether it will upset me or not. I'm glad they don't know how to react. It means they've not had loss.

"We can talk about it over ice cream," I say to Gemma.

"Ice cream," Kaitlyn belts out, and we both laugh.

"Nothing gets by her." I shake my head. "Unless you have other plans," I say, hoping she doesn't.

"I do," she says. A ridiculous sense of disappointment sits heavy in my gut and I work to ignore it. "But," she says brightly, holding up an index finger. "Ice cream first." A smile reaches her dark eyes when they meet mine. "It's been too long, Callan," she says in a soft voice. "Let's get caught up."

"I'd love that."

"Yay," Kaitlyn says, her hand sliding into mine. "Swing me, Daddy."

I pick her up under the arms, and give her a swing, and she squeals in delight. I set her down and she grabs my hand and Gemma's. "Now both swing me."

"Kaitlyn—" I begin, wanting to set boundaries when it comes to other people.

"It's okay," Gemma says, and we both take one arm up high, so it doesn't pop from the socket as we swing her.

"That was fun," Kaitlyn says as we reach the car. She hops into the back to buckle herself in, and I glance around to see what Gemma is driving.

"I walk to school," she says. "I bought a townhouse a few blocks away."

"Oh, nice. I didn't realize." I pull her door open for her. "Ride me." What the fuck. I give a quick shake of my head at my blunder. "I mean ride *with* me," I say quickly.

"I know what you meant," she says, mature enough not to needle me as she slides into the car and sets her papers on the back seat beside Kaitlyn. None of the guys at the station would have let that go, and when I say guys, I mean the female fighters. I love them all dearly, like family, but they love to *ride* my ass—as in harass me relentlessly, all in good fun of course. I get a whiff of her scent as she settles in my passenger seat, and I tug my hair, closing the door behind her.

Ride me?

Really, Callan?

Shit, it was a simple slip, but now that I've said it, I kind of can't stop thinking about it. Me in bed, sweet Gemma on top of me. My dick twitches as I circle the car and I clench my teeth and work to purify my thoughts. Yeah, the guys are right. I do need to get laid. I never was the kind of guy to sleep around, but maybe it's time for a one-night stand. Not with Gemma, of course. We're just friends. Yeah, sure she was cute in high school, but four years of college later, combined with a couple years of teaching, well, let's just say she turned into a beautiful woman. I can't understand why she's still single. Maybe her break-up with Brad was recent, and she's not ready to get back into the game. I can understand that.

I back out of my spot and head toward Boston Common. Fifteen minutes later we're walking through the park, eating our dripping ice-cream cones. Joggers run the path around the park, as families picnic, or play with their pets.

"I'm going to teach Gilbert how to fetch," Kaitlyn states unambiguously, and Gemma stifles a chuckle when I glance at her.

"That'll be a neat trick," I say, and zero in on the big stain of ice cream on Gemma's face. "You have a bit..." I reach for her face, and she jerks backward. Whoa. What the hell? "Sorry, you just have some ice cream on your face."

"Right, okay," she says, her eyes big as she swipes her mouth with a napkin.

Fuck, I've been the first on the scene in many situations, including domestic abuse. If I didn't know better... Hell, I don't know better. A burst of protectiveness goes through me. "Everything okay, Gemma?"

"Yeah, sure," she says, all bright-eyed. "You just startled me." She turns her attention to Kaitlyn. "Will you be at the Boys and Girls club this summer?" she asks, and I don't miss the fast switch in conversations.

"Will I be, Daddy?"

"You bet you will be. But next week you're going to stay with Grammy and Grampy, remember?" I say, my stomach coiled tight. Is someone hurting Gemma? If so, I'd like to meet them, and introduce my fist to their face.

"Grammy has a bird," she says.

"What kind of bird?" Gemma asks.

Kaitlyn holds her hands a couple inches apart. "It's a perky." She rolls her eyes. "I like him but he sings a lot."

"Parakeet," I correct. In the distance I spot fellow fire-fighter Colin and the guys playing frisbee. I waved as we pass, and inside Gemma's purse her phone starts ringing—a ringtone I don't recognize, which probably means its personalized and she knows who's calling. She tenses and ignores the chime. It keeps on ringing, the caller as tenacious as a six-year-old.

"You going to get that?" I ask.

"No," she says flatly.

I shove my hands into my pockets, and cast her a sidelong glance, aware of the tightness in her shoulders, her rapid intake of breath. "Want me to get it for you?"

"No, it's..." Her head slowly lifts, her eyes filled with something that looks like despair when they latch on mine.

I come to an abrupt halt. "Jesus, Gemma, what is it?"

2

GEMMA

Dammit, dammit, dammit.

I never meant to react when Callan reached for my face, or again just now when my phone started ringing. He's a smart guy, one of the smartest I know, and he's a firefighter to boot. Guys like him, first responders, they're used to dealing with those in a crisis. Not that I'm in a crisis. Not anymore, anyway. Or maybe I still am.

All I know is my ex is going to be at the annual family get-together this weekend, and he's the last person on the face of the earth I want to see. I'd tried to break it off with him numerous times over the last couple of years, but he always apologized for his behavior, always insisting he'd change. I'm a cliché, I know. But it doesn't change the fact that I'm still a little afraid of him, and his violent outbursts. He's never laid a hand on me, but his threatening nature, always putting me down, and rough handling me in the bedroom, broke me a little, or a lot. I shake my head and push down the memories.

Honestly, I'd skip the reunion altogether, if it weren't for my parents. Dad's health hasn't been great and I don't see them enough as it is. They're both looking forward to seeing me and what they'd like most is to see me back with Brad. The man could win an Oscar for his performances when he's not behind closed doors.

"It's my mother," I say, and keep walking.

He continues on with me, slowing his strides to match mine, and I look straight ahead, but that doesn't mean I can't feel his eyes drilling into me. God, I wish I wasn't such an easy read. We might not have seen each other for a while, but Callan was always nice to me, always protective of those in our group.

"You don't like your mother?" he asks.

That pulls a laugh from my throat, and eases some of the tension in my shoulders. "No, of course I do." I take my last bite of ice cream and wipe my mouth. "It's just, ugh, it's the annual Davis weekend."

"You lost me there."

"Once a year, we have a big gathering at my parents place. They moved to the Cape after I graduated high school." We make our way back to his car, and I continue with, "I mean, I'm looking forward to seeing everyone. Mostly."

"Who is it you don't want to see?" he asks, straight up. Leave it to Callan to get to the bottom of matters.

My body bumps his as we walk, and I move back quickly. Men like Callan, big, strong, powerful. Those are the kind of guys I go out of my way to avoid. Callan, however, he's not like my ex. He's always been sweet, and I probably shouldn't be thinking about him naked. Clearly, it's been too long since I've been touched by a nice guy, a guy who would never threaten to hurt me after a bad day at work—or even a good day.

"My ex is going to be there," I say and scrunch up my nose. "Awkward, and all," I add to cover the truth.

"Ah," he says. "I take it the breakup wasn't mutual then."

"I broke it off with him, and no, not mutual." My heart pounds a little faster. "He's still messaging me, and he wants to get back together," I say, wondering why I'm telling him any of this. I don't talk about my ex, don't even want to think about him. I guess with the weekend reunion tomorrow, it's hard not to think about him. Not only am I thinking about him, the jerk is also invading my dreams. Every night for this past week, I've been waking up in a cold sweat. His folks are old friends of my parents. They were all so happy when we got together. None of them can understand the breakup, and I'm not about to drag my parents into my problems. I just wanted a clean break and to put it all behind me

"Is he harassing you?" he finally asks, pulling my thoughts back. I swallow as we reach the car and Kaitlyn jumps into the back seat, buckling herself into her booster seat.

"Let's just say he doesn't like to take no for an answer."

His steps slow and the muscles along his jaw clench. "Is he hurting you, Gemma?"

"No, no," I say quickly. "I just wish he'd get it in his head that we're not getting back together."

Callan pauses, his gaze moving over my face. "Ever think of a restraining order?"

A humorless laugh catches in my throat. "He's a cop, Callan. It complicates things." I can't even imagine how much he, or his fellow officers, would harass me if I went to the courts. I've been around his buddies enough to know they stick together no matter what. At the end of the day, I'm physically fine, but it's the mental abuse, his possessiveness that frightens me. Avoiding him has been my best course of action, and that's worked so far. With the weekend coming, he's been reaching out to me again. Changing my number and making it private hasn't stopped him. Which just goes to show me how much power he has.

"It shouldn't complicate things," Callan says softly.

"You're right, it shouldn't." I open my door and slide in. Callan stands there for a moment, his brow furrowed as he scrubs his chin. My insides tighten. I've already said too much, and to Callan at that. He has enough problems of his own. He doesn't need to be taking on mine, or worrying about me. "It's okay, Callan. Everything is okay. I'm sure the weekend will be fine."

He nods, but doesn't look convinced as he circles the car and jumps in. He turns the engine over and backs up.

"Daddy, can we have pizza for dinner?"

He glances at Kaitlyn in the rearview mirror. "Sounds like a good idea," he says, the muscles in his shoulders tight, like he's still trying to work through what I shouldn't have just told him.

"Can Miss Davis have pizza with us?"

"Oh, honey, that's okay—" I begin but Callan cuts me off.

"I do make a mean pizza," Callan says. "Three-time champion at the station." He blows on his knuckles and shines them on his shirt. I grin, happy to see the playful Callan back.

"Wait, you *make* pizza? Like, homemade pizza? Not frozen from a box?"

"I'm pretty good in the kitchen, I'll have you know."

Kaitlyn rubs her belly. "He puts extra cheese on it for me."

Back in high school, Callan was the school's jock. Totally into fitness—he's still physically fit—and while he always ate well, I never saw him as the kind of guy to enjoy cooking.

"When did you get so good in the kitchen?" I ask and instantly regret it. Ugh. Sometimes I need to engage my brain before my mouth. He's been on his own with Kaitlyn for two years. The man learned to cook out of necessity. "I didn't mean. I'm just—"

He laughs to make light of it and I'm grateful. "You're coming for pizza then?" he asks

"How can I say no to extra cheese?" I look straight ahead and reclip my hair. "Is it true, that at the fire station, you guys all cook for one another?"

"Yup, it's true."

"And you have competitions?"

"I wouldn't call it a competition." He lifts his head and his chest puffs up, a playful grin on his face. "Not when the guys don't really stand a chance against me."

I laugh at that, feeling so much lighter. I love how he puts me at ease. "Wow, that's some ego you've got there, my friend."

He grins. "Only because I can back it up."

"I bet you can," I say and before I can help myself my gaze drops to take in the lovely bulge in his crotch. He shifts, and my gaze flies back to his. Oh my God, I was just checking out my friend's crotch, and he caught me doing it.

Instead of calling me on it, and for that I'm grateful, he says, "I can give you a tour of the station if you like."

"Yeah, actually that might be fun. Maybe we can arrange something with the Boys and Girls club in the coming weeks."

"That would be fun, Daddy," Kaitlyn says, but I can only imagine she's been there numerous times.

"I'll look into it. As the top chef, I have a lot of pull."

Chuckling at his sense of humor, I sit back and relax into the seat as he drives us to his house. He coasts into the driveway and as soon as we come to a complete stop, Kaitlyn unbuckles, jumps from the back seat, and runs to the small group of kids skipping in the next driveway.

"She's such a happy little girl," I say to Callan, my heart warming at the image of the kids playing. It reminds me of my own childhood, and my two older sisters. They too became teachers, following in our mother's footsteps, and they'll be home with their husbands and kids for the gathering.

He smiles, his look distant, like he's remembering happier times, and my stomach clenches. It must be hard to watch his little girl grow up without a mother, to think about a mother missing out on all her child's life. Wanting to lighten things, I reach for my door handle and say, "So what's the secret to this pizza, and please don't tell me it's lard."

He grins. "Come on, I'll teach you."

"Really, you'll share your big secret?"

"I think my secret is safe with you, Gemma."

I lift my chin an inch. "Maybe I'll slip it to one of the guys at the station when we're on tour. Knock your ego down a peg or two."

"Then I'd say you're forgetting something."

I narrow my eyes. What on earth is he talking about. "What am I forgetting?"

He throws his arm around me, and a quiver goes through me. He jerks it back, clearly mistaking my reaction this time and I can't blame him. "Sorry. I didn't mean—"

"It's okay," I say. "You just surprised me earlier, that's all." It's true he did. I know Callan would never hurt me, but he doesn't need to know that Brad would put his fist up to my face in anger, just to see me flinch. I hate how long it took me to end it. I'm ashamed by it, to be honest, though I shouldn't be. For those who don't understand abuse, staying can sometimes be easier. It takes courage to leave. Guys like Brad prey on that fear.

My gaze moves over his handsome face, his gorgeous blue eyes, and I can't help but wonder if my secret is safe with him. Then again, what good would come out of telling him about my ex's possessive behavior, the violence he could barely keep on simmer? A guy like Callan Ward, well, he'd likely go after him, and that would bring nothing but trouble to his family and loved ones.

"What am I forgetting?" I ask, bringing the conversation back around.

"You helped me pick out Zoe's promise ring. It killed you to keep it a secret from her. But you did."

I smile at that. "I swear I was ready to burst."

"Yeah, you were like a great big hippopotamus holding its breath for weeks."

I put one hand on my hip and glare at him. "Excuse me?"

"It was a compliment," he says with a laugh.

I shake my head. "Yes, how could I mistake being called a hippo as anything other than a compliment."

His head drops, hangs low in shame. "I've clearly been hanging around six-year olds too much."

"You definitely need some adult company, Callan."

"That I do."

I resist the urge to ask what else he might need as he starts up the driveway and my gaze drops to his very fine ass, showcased by low slung jeans. I follow him up the walkway, and he opens the door and gestures for me to enter. My heart jumps into my throat when I step into the entranceway and glance around. The house is warm, comfy, and a bit untidy, but everywhere I look, I see love, and laughter—pictures of family, of a wife that hadn't changed in two years. Because she's gone. The last time I was here was four years ago, when they bought the place and had a housewarming party.

His late wife Zoe still lives on here, and I'm not sure whether that is a good or bad thing. I haven't seen our old group in a long time. Zoe was the glue that kept us together. Has Callan even been with anyone since she's been gone? I'm thinking no. All signs point to it. He did just admit that he needed adult company. Zoe would have wanted him to move on with his life. Of that I have no doubt.

"Just like I remember it." My voice is low, barely a whisper, as my heart thumps a little harder against my ribcage.

His throat makes a sound as he swallows. "Don't mind the mess. I'm not much of a housekeeper."

"It's homey," I say to him and he gives me a grateful smile.

"I hire a nanny for Kaitlyn in the summers. She starts when Kaitlyn gets back from her week at her grandparents. She tidies up while she's here, but for ten months of the year, it's a bit of a mess."

He gives me a smile, but that's when it occurs to me. He might look put together, but underneath it all, the man is held together by frayed stitches. God, I didn't even know what kind of shape he's been in. My heart sits heavy in my chest. What kind of friend have I been, not to know Callan was living in a time capsule, and simply going from day to day?

"Who takes care of Kaitlyn during the school year when you're on shift?" I follow him to the kitchen and he removes a stack of papers from the chair and gestures for me to sit.

"She does the Boys and Girls club after school, but on the nights I'm working, she usually goes to one of the grandparents' places."

"You have a great support system." There isn't a lot of stability for Kaitlyn, going from home to home, but I guess they're doing what they have to do to get by. A measure of guilt gnaws at me. I should have been there for him over the years. Well, I'm here now. Maybe I can help him move on with his future.

"Yeah, I do," he says but it's what he's not saying that tightens my throat. While he has numerous people there for him and Kaitlyn, no one can take the place of his wife, and I have to agree.

"Drink?" he asks as children's laughter trickles in through the open windows and fills the house. A smile tugs at the corners of my mouth. When Brad and I first got together he was so damn charming and I used to dream about having a family with him. Now that I'm single, recuperating from an abusive relationship, I just want to keep a low profile and try to find myself again. As much as I want kids, I'm not sure I see it happening.

He opens the fridge and leans in. "Wine or beer?" I stand, unable to sit idle while someone serves me and step up behind him to see what he's offering.

"If we're having pizza, I think that calls for a beer," I say.

"I knew there was a reason I always liked you," he says and turns around, bumping into me again. I stumble backward, but he slides his free hand around my waist. The other is holding two beers. He pulls me to him and I become acutely aware of the strength in his body as it presses against mine. "Sorry, Gemma. I didn't know you were standing there."

"We have to stop meeting like this," I tease, but dammit, my voice holds a hint of arousal that I pray he doesn't pick up on.

He laughs. "You're kind of stealthy."

"It's always been one of my finer qualities. It's at the top of my resume, actually. Bachelor of education, pianist, stealthy," I tease. Why isn't he letting me go? Better yet, why don't I want him to? "It's a skill that helped me get a job teaching English to seventh graders."

"The school needed a stealthy teacher for that, did they?"

I open my eyes wide in mock surprise. "You clearly have no idea how sneaky teenagers can be with their phones, especially when it comes to cheating."

He arches a brow, and his clean soapy scent fills my lungs.

"Ah, so you have the ability to sneak up on that and catch them in the act."

"That's right."

"You'll have to teach me that. Kaitlyn is six going on thirteen."

I chuckle, but it comes out rough and hoarse. "I'm sorry to say it's not teachable. You're either born with it or you're not. Sadly, I think you lack the skill, Callan. You're too big to be stealthy."

"Too big, huh?" He angles his head. "Wait, is that a sideways compliment, like the hippo?"

His heat moves through me, trickles through my blood and settles between my legs. My God, what is going on with me? This is Callan. I can't go there with him. He's not over his late wife, and never will be—which is unfortunate because everyone deserves happiness—and the last thing he's likely looking for is a relationship. A brief affair, however.

Wait, what?

"Not a sideways compliment, Callan. It's a compliment. I remember every girl wanted to be with you back in high school."

Myself included.

His hand slides from my back, leaving cold where there was once warmth. Okay, Gemma, that's your cue to move backward, put a measure of space between our bodies.

Why the hell aren't I moving back?

Because Callan is sweet, hot and fun, and I haven't been around a man like that since...Callan. Still, he's my late friend's husband—a widower—and I shouldn't be thinking inappropriate thoughts, like putting my hands on his hard, naked body, touching his flesh and caressing his hard muscles with my fingertips. Or him touching me in return. Since I broke things off with Brad, I've not looked at another man, haven't wanted to. But there's something so incredibly safe and warm about Callan. I don't know. Everything about him draws me in. Probably because he's big and strong, and comes with his own gravitational pull.

"That's not true," he says.

I lift my finger and start checking things off. "Captain of the football team, good student, always nice to everyone. Even the new girls in town. But you were with..." Shit. Shit. Shit. What is the matter with me? I shouldn't be bringing up painful memories for him. I back up and fall into my chair.

"I was with Zoe," he says, his body tight.

I shake my head and mentally kick myself. "Yeah, sorry, I didn't mean to bring her up."

He drops down into the chair next to me and pulls it close until our knees are almost touching. "It's okay to talk about her, Gemma. I like that people remember her."

I blink through the water in my eyes. "Really?"

"Yes, really."

"Okay, I just didn't know." Without even realizing it, I lean into him, and put my hand on his face, his late day shadow prickly against my palm. "She was the best, Callan."

His nod is slow, his voice tight when he says, "I know."

The front door flings open and Callan pushes to his feet and turns toward his daughter as she rushes down the hallway. "I need a drink," Kaitlyn says.

"Right," Callan says, and grabs a drink glass from the cupboard. He turns on the tap and runs it until it's cold.

Kaitlyn glances around. "Is the pizza ready?" Callan hands her a tall glass of water and she gulps it. My hand goes to my stomach as I watch her, a sense of longing building inside me.

"Not yet," Callan says.

"Can Liam have pizza with us?" she asks as she hands the drink glass back.

Callan shrugs. "I guess. If it's okay with his mother."

"It's okay with her," Kaitlyn says and swipes the back of

her hand over her mouth, wiping away the traces of ice cream and water on her face.

"How do you know that?" Callan asks.

"We already asked her."

He arches a brow at me. "You okay with Liam coming over?"

"Of course. I love kids and two is much easier than thirty."

"I can't even imagine." Callan laughs and shakes his head. "Fine, he can come for pizza. I'll call you both when it's ready. Remember the rules. Do not go on the road."

She gives an exasperated sigh. "I'm not a baby."

"Oh, I know," Callan says and cracks the beers. The door slams shut as he fills our glasses and hands one to me.

"You do have your hands full."

"Like I said, six going on thirteen."

"Good thing she has a big strong daddy to frighten all the boys off."

"A big strong daddy who owns a gun."

I laugh at that. "I pity the boys who ask her out when she's older."

"You should," he jokes and opens his pantry. He pulls out flour and sugar and some other things, and I kick my legs out as I watch him. Warmth moves through me, probably from the beer—I am such a light-weight—but the truth is, I haven't relaxed in a long time. Everything about this place screams love, home and heart. It's so easy to be here.

With all the ingredients laid out, he plugs his kettle in, picks his beer back up and steps toward me. He holds his glass up in salute.

"What are we celebrating?" I ask.

"How about old friendships," he says, bending to tap his glass to mine. I try not to notice his closeness or the way it overwhelms me. For a brief second I consider his overprotective nature. Brad might think twice about harassing me if Callan was by my side. Yeah, Brad would probably tuck tail and run the other way—bully that he is. Not that I'm about to ask Callan to come to the Cape for the weekend, or pretend to be my boyfriend for the duration. That's completely ludicrous, right?

Or is it?

3

CALLAN

"Okay, Liam, time to get you home," I say after we all finish eating. I stand and take our plates to the sink.

Kaitlyn pouts. "I don't want him to go."

"You have to get packed for you grandparents, Kaitlyn, remember?" Her eyes light up. "But first we walk Liam home."

Gemma wipes her mouth with the paper napkin, stands and brings a few more dishes to the counter. "I can stay here and help Kaitlyn get packed while you go."

I hesitate for a second. "Are you sure? I don't want to put you out."

Too bad. I'd love to put out.

My God, who said that?

"I want Miss Davis to help me pack," Kaitlyn says.

Gemma reaches for Kaitlyn's hand and my heart twists in an odd little way as my daughter slides her hand into Gemma's. "I really don't mind."

"Okay," I say as Liam jumps from his chair.

"See you later, Kaitlyn," he says, and walks to the door.

"You guys can hang out again when we get back," I tell Liam as we leave the house. I walk two houses down, and he rushes inside. His mother pokes her head out.

"Thanks for having him for dinner," Danielle says to me.

"No problem. He's a great kid." She has an odd little grin on her face. "Something wrong?" I ask.

"No, I just...well, Kaitlyn said Miss. Davis was having pizza with you guys."

I nod. No hiding your business with a six-year-old. "Miss Davis, or rather Gemma, is an old friend of mine. We go way back."

She leans against her doorway, like she's in no hurry to leave and normally I'd spend a few minutes talking. Tonight however, I'm a little anxious to get back home and it's not because I've left my daughter with someone new.

"I think that's nice," she says, and I stifle a groan. Cripes, come tomorrow morning I'm sure I'll be the talk of the neighborhood.

"We're just old friends," I tell her.

"Well, you never know," she says.

"What don't I know?" I ask and wish I hadn't.

Her smile is coy, and a bit hopeful. "What starts inno-cently enough..."

I hold my hand up to stop her. "Night, Danielle," I say and turn. Having Gemma at the house has no doubt raised suspicions, considering I've not had a woman who wasn't family, or a babysitter, or a firefighter at the house in...ever. Basically, I've not had a woman at the house that was there for me.

Whoa, what?

Gemma is not there for me, per se. We're just old friends getting caught up and I wanted to spend more time with her after getting a bad feeling about her ex-boyfriend.

"Just think about it," she calls after me and in my heart, I know she means well. The people in my neighborhood are kind and caring, always wanting to introduce me to their friends, or relatives, but my personal life is my own business and I plan to keep it that way.

Music seeps from the open windows and reaches my ears as I approach the house, and breath leaves my lungs in a whoosh as old memories come rushing back. I grip the paint-chipped handrail and hold for a second, the music taking me back to happier times—when Zoe was the one at that piano. Kaitlyn's squeal of laugher rises over the music and wraps around my heart.

I suck in a fast breath and dart up the three steps. I round the corner and find Gemma and Kaitlyn at the piano. The sight stabs my heart. Gemma's head lifts, and her smile falls from her face the second she sees me.

"Sorry, we got sidetracked." She stands quickly. "I'll help Kaitlyn pack and get going."

I shake my head and put my hand on her shoulder to stop her. "Why don't you two keep playing? I'll pack Kaitlyn's stuff."

"Thank you, Daddy," Kaitlyn yells out.

"Are you sure?"

"I'm positive."

She gives a small nod and tentatively sits down again. I dash up the stairs, and happy music fills the house and my soul as I pack my daughter's bag and run the tub. I head back downstairs and find the two laughing as Gemma teaches her basic notes.

"All set for your bath kiddo."

"I don't want to."

"You run up and have your bath," Gemma says as she checks her watch, and I ignore the heavy feeling in my chest. "I have to get going anyway."

"Give us a few minutes," I say. "Her bath won't take long.

Why don't you pour yourself a glass of wine, and flick the TV on? We haven't really had a chance to catch up."

She hesitates, a line in her forehead as Kaitlyn jumps up and dashes up the stairs. "I suppose." She snorts out a humorless laugh. "I don't really have to rush home for anything. It's not a school night."

"It's settled then. Grab a beer or a wine, and I'll just be a few minutes."

I stand there for a second as she stands and saunters into the kitchen. The second she's out of my sight, I hurry upstairs, and Kaitlyn is undressing for her bath.

"Daddy," she begins as I help her into the warm water.

"Yeah."

"I really like Miss Davis. She's nice."

"She is nice, isn't she? Did you know that we used to go to school together? Many years ago."

Her eyes grow wide. "Really?"

"Yup, just like you and Liam are in the same class, Miss Davis and I were too."

"That's funny."

"I suppose it is."

"Can she have dinner with us every night?"

"I don't know about that. She has her own place and she has things to do."

"I like that she's going to be at the Boys and Girls club. She's always nice to me."

"That's good to know."

"I don't like Mrs. Follows. She's grumpy."

I bite back a chuckle. There's not a thing wrong with Mrs. Follows, she's just older and is a little more regimented than the volunteer teachers at the club.

I give her a washcloth and she proceeds to clean herself. Once she's finished soaping up, she rinses off and I wrap a big towel around her and lift her from the tub. She squeals as I hold her up over my head and fly her to her bed.

I make an airplane sound as I lower her to her bed, and she tugs on the pajamas I laid out for her.

Once she's dressed, I read her a book, give her a kiss and leave her room. In the hall I take a big breath, and I can't figure out why I'm suddenly nervous about the idea of spending alone time with Gemma.

The soft sound of the TV reaches my ears as I descend the steps and her mess of hair, now unclipped falls down her back as she does something with her phone.

"Hey," I say quietly, and she turns, a glass of white wine in her hand and a beer on the table for me.

"I opened a bottle," she says, setting her phone down. "I hope you don't mind."

"Not at all." I glance at the TV. "What are you watching?"

"Not much on. Found a chick flick." She crinkles her nose, an apologetic look on her face. "Probably not your thing, right?"

"There are one of two things you'll find on in this place. Cartoons, or big action flicks."

"I'll change it." She reaches for the remote, but I cross the room and put my hand over hers to stop her. The second our hands connect, a burst of heat zaps through me, and there's nothing I can do to stop my dick from twitching. What the hell is going on with me?

"It's okay, we can watch it," I tell her and her dark eyes, full of something that looks like desire, something that is no doubt reflected in mine, go wide.

"Are you sure?"

"It will do me good to watch something other than explosions and violence."

"You don't get that enough in your day-to-day life?" she asks.

I laugh, but it comes out sounding rough and tortured. "Apparently not."

She snuggles back into the sofa. "Okay then. This is one of my favorites."

I pick up my beer and take a long pull from the bottle. It's cold and refreshing but the only thing that's going to cool my dick down is if I dip it into the brew. I sit back, and catch a sidelong glance of her, a small smile on her face as she focuses her attention on the TV. When I recognize the male lead's voice—I'm used to seeing him in action flicks—I turn. "What are we watching, anyway?"

"The Proposal. It's my favorite."

"What's your favorite? The show or Ryan Reynolds?" I ask and she grins.

Outside, the sun sets on the horizon, and the streets go quiet as everyone settles themselves in for the night. I jump up to close the window and sneeze when a breeze blows in.

"You must be getting a cold," Gemma says.

"Allergies. It's that time of year. I better start taking my meds."

I grab another beer, sit back down and when a commercial comes on, I turn to Gemma. "What do you guys do at this Davis weekend, anyway?"

She turns my way, and when I notice her glass is empty, I jump up, and get the bottle from the kitchen. As I refill her glass she says, "Oh, we have a barbecue, swim, play games."

"Sounds like fun."

"It usually is. Just..."

"Brad?"

"Yeah?"

She turns back to the commercial, effectively cutting me off, and I let it go for the time being. Her ex is a sore spot, and I suspect there is more going on than she wants to say. I sit next to her, fully aware of her presence for the rest of the movie. It's hard to concentrate when she chuckles or makes those little breathy sounds when something romantic happens. She's definitely a romantic at heart.

The final credits come on and Gemma flicks the TV off. She exhales slowly, and that's when I realize I can't drive her home for two reasons. One, my daughter is asleep and even if I did call the neighbor over to watch her for a few minutes, two, I've had a couple drinks.

"I should get going. I have to pack tonight too and head to the Cape." She gives a very unenthusiastic, "Yay," then shakes her head and groans. "I love my family, I really do. I hate that I'm not looking forward to going."

"It's understandable. Your ex will be there and that makes it awkward."

"His family, my family, they all go way back," she says with a frown. "I just wish he understood that we're over. I stayed with him too long as it was," she mumbles, and her eyes go wide, like she said too much, but I'm beginning to get a clearer picture of Brad here, and I don't like it one little bit.

"I was just thinking." I glance out at the dark night. "Maybe you should stay the night." Her eyes go big again and I quickly clarify. "I just mean it's late, and," I point to my empty beer bottles. "I didn't think before I had a couple drinks. I'm not used to having women over and driving them home."

"I can get an Uber," she says, and stretches out, but she doesn't look like she's in any hurry to leave.

"Yeah, but you know. I'm not really comfortable with that. If I can't see you home safely, and personally, then I'd rather you'd stay." I stifle a sneeze again, and gesture toward the stairs. "I can drive you home in the morning, on the way to Kaitlyn's grandparents' house."

"It is late," she says. "I don't really have any reason to rush home." She looks down for a moment, and I sense the loneliness in her. I understand it, perfectly.

"I have a spare toothbrush and some clothes you can wear." Her face pales and I instantly realize she's thinking I mean Zoe's. "My clothes," I say. "They'll be big on you, but no one will see, but you."

"I guess," she says. "You don't think Kaitlyn will mind...or get the wrong idea?"

"She's six. The only ones who might get the wrong idea are my neighbors and believe me they'd be thrilled."

I stand and pull her up with me.

"Thrilled?"

"They're always trying to set me up. When I dropped Liam off, his mother basically gave me the winky-wink and thumbs up."

She laughs. "I guess we're definitely going to give them something to talk about."

"Big time." She follows me up the stairs and into my bedroom. I pull open my dresser and grab her a clean t-shirt. I toss it on the bed and grab a pair of sweat shorts with a drawstring from my closet. I hand them to her.

"Did you tell them we were just friends?" she asks as she stifles a yawn. "That we go way back?"

I snort. "Yeah, but they have their own theory on that."

"Oh, like friends with benefits," she says with a laugh that sounds a little hoarse, and my dick twitches as it encourages me to go for it. I'm not looking for a relationship, and she doesn't seem to be, either. Friends with benefits, however.

Whoa, where did that come from?

"Let them talk, Gemma. Maybe it will stop them from trying to set me up."

She picks the clothes up and holds them against her body. "All right then. Let's give them something to talk about." Her smile falls off. "I don't mean literally. I just mean—"

"I know what you mean," I say. I back out of the room. "I'll leave a spare toothbrush out for you and in the morning, I'm making waffles."

She laughs, totally getting the joke. "That'll do donkey," she says to my reference to the children's movie.

Her laugh follows me down the hall as I make a quick trip to the bathroom, take a couple of allergy pills and check on Kaitlyn. I drop down onto the sofa and sprawl out. I wake up sniffing from allergies, and completely foggy-brained, going to the kitchen for a drink of water. Still half asleep I groggily climb the stairs and crawl back into bed.

GEMMA

A strange noise in the distance pulls me awake. My lids fly open, my heart beating double time in my chest as the last fragment of my erotic dream drifts away. I glance around the dark room and try to get my bearings.

Callan's room.

I relax against the soft mattress as my hot body practically vibrates, my dream coming back to me in heated flashes. I close my eyes again, wanting to go back to my fantasy world as the images play out in my mind's eye. I honestly can't believe I was dreaming of my old friend, his mouth on my body, kissing a path to the needy juncture between my legs. A low groan crawls out of my throat, and a movement beside me has me going still.

What is going on?

I stiffen at first, thinking I'm imagining things. Maybe I hadn't run into Callan today—literally. Maybe that was just wishful thinking and I'm actually back in my own bed, and it's Brad shifting beside me. A violent quake goes through me, and a burst of panic grips my stomach as air wheezes from my lungs.

"Gemma?"

The sound of Callan's voice instantly puts me at ease. I inhale a relieved breath and place my hands over my chest to still my racing heart. Wait, what is he doing in bed with me?

"Gemma, are you okay?" The nightstand lamp flicks on, bathing the room in soft light. Callan's blue eyes narrow in on me. He blinks, then frowns as he glances around his dark room. "How did I get here?"

I laugh softly. "I don't know. Maybe you were sleepwalking and habit brought you to this bed."

His lips curl in a soft smile as he pushes the blankets off his shoulders. "I took a couple allergy pills. That's probably exactly what happened. I'm sorry. I'll get out of here." He shifts and the blankets hover around his stomach, giving me a view of his near naked body.

Sweet baby Jesus.

"Wait," he says. "Something woke me up. Were you trembling, or talking in your sleep?"

"Just a dream," I say. "I'm okay now."

"Maybe more like a nightmare," he states, but he'd be wrong. The dream was erotic, the nightmare happened when I was wide awake, thinking Brad was next to me. He makes a move to get up, and I'm instantly disappointed. He's a big guy, but he radiates comfort and safety.

"Callan," I say softly, and tentatively reach for him. I pull my hand back, and he glances at it, aware I was reaching for him.

"Yeah."

"Do you think...um...you could stay for a little bit?"

He goes perfectly still for a moment and I berate myself. What a stupid thing to ask. I shouldn't be asking the man for his comfort. I shouldn't be asking him for anything. He's dealing with enough in life as it is.

"I'm sorry. I shouldn't have—" I begin, but stop when he puts his hand on my arm.

"I can stay," he says and drops back down, turning to his side. He goes up on one elbow and rests his head in his palm. "Were you having a nightmare?"

"Actually, the nightmare was when I was awake. I felt a movement beside me and for a brief second I thought it was Brad." I shift beneath the sheet and that's when I realize I'm dressed only in my bra and underwear. Callan's clothes were so big on me, I was worried I'd strangle myself in my sleep. I sink deeper into the bedding and tug the sheets to my neck, leaving my arms outside the bedding, braced at my sides.

"That frightened you, didn't it?" he says, like he's completely aware of the life I lived with Brad.

"A little," I say. I'm not sure what's making me open up. Perhaps it's the late hour, or maybe the fortress around my heart is still asleep. Or perhaps it's simply because this is Callan, a damaged man, but a guy I can trust. He's so kind and sweet, so easy to open up to. "Things weren't great between us."

"I figured as much. I'm sorry." He reaches out, lightly runs a finger along my arm, and a small quiver goes through me. His brow bunches with worry. "Did he hurt you, Gemma?"

A little moan I have no control over catches in my throat and Callan's gaze flashes to mine. "Not really."

"What does not really mean?" he asks, a dark edge to his voice.

"He never hit me or anything. He was aggressive and threatened me, and sometimes..."

"Sometimes what?" he asks, moving even closer, until I feel his warm breath on my face.

"Sometimes, I don't know, I guess in bed, he could get a little rough."

"You don't like it rough," he says, a statement, not a question. I get it, some women like it rough, I'm just not one of them, and I'm not sure Brad's brand of rough is what any woman would like anyway. It was almost...possessive, like it held a deeper warning.

"It actually scared me. He was pretty intimidating and domineering, at times."

"He was a fucking bully."

"Yeah."

"You've voiced this?" he asks, but he's not victim-blaming here, like some do. Some would say it's my fault. I didn't fight enough, or stand up to him. It's easy for them to say it. It's different when you're in the situation.

"I did."

"I'm sorry, Gemma. Your ex was a real douche-bag."

"Yeah, he was," I say a bit breathless as his naked leg touches mine.

"I'm glad you found the courage and left him. I know that's not easy."

"You do?" I say, but yeah, of course he does.

"I'm a first responder. I come across many different situations in my line of work."

My heart beats a little fast, and honestly, I feel a bit lighter sharing my painful past with Callan. "Thanks for understanding," I say. "I don't think most really understand."

His finger trails higher, a gentle sweep to my shoulder. He draws tiny circles, and his tender touch travels through my body, settling deep between my legs. My God, what is going on here?

"I'd love to have five minutes with him. Let him pick on someone his own size."

"I don't want you involved, Callan. It's over. I'll face him this weekend, and make sure he knows it. We won't ever be alone, and my family will be there. I'll be safe."

"Okay," he says and shifts closer. I don't flinch, but I do suck in a fast breath.

"I'd never do anything to hurt you, Gemma, physically or emotionally."

"I know," I say my voice coming out a little squeaky. "I trust you, Callan. You're one of the good guys."

"I'm glad you trust me," he says, his voice an octave lower. "And just so you know, if I was ever going to touch you, I'd be gentle. But I'd never touch you if you didn't want me to," he says and as I take in the heat in his eyes, I understand he's asking me a question.

Oh. My. God. Callan is asking if I want him to touch me.

I turn on my side, and he removes his hand from my arm. "If I was ever to touch you, I'd want you to want it, too," I say. "I'd want you to like it."

He nods, and takes a deep breath. "It's been a long time since I've been touched, Gemma. Since Zoe. I've not...I haven't been able...I'm not sure I..."

He doesn't finish, so I try to fill in the blanks. "I know, me neither," I say, and my heart beats faster, my brain hardly able to believe what I'm about to suggest. "Maybe we should just try and see."

"What do you mean?" he asks.

"I can touch you, and you can let me know if you want it. Let's just be open and honest with each other."

"I like that idea," he says and as he gazes at me, I get that he likes me, too. Good, because I like him, the warmth between my legs is a damn good indication of that.

"If I touched you here, would you want it, or like it?" I reach out and put my hand on his hot chest, and he sucks in a fast breath as his heart thunders beneath my palm.

"Yeah, I like that," he says, sounding as breathless as I do.

My blankets shift a little, exposing the lace on my bra. "My turn," he says, and his throat makes a sound when he swallows. He looks into my eyes and that's when I get that he's waiting for a response, asking permission, and my heart wobbles a little. My God, he is such a sweet guy.

"Okay," I say.

He reaches out, and puts his finger on the curve of my jaw. His eyes meet mine and I answer the question lingering there.

"I like it," I say.

"How about this," he slides his finger down my throat, in a slow, tender way that teases all my erogenous zones. "So far so good?" he asks.

"Yes," I say, my voice nothing more than a needy whisper.

He continues downward, my skin on fire everywhere he touches, burning in a way it has never burned before, and I like it. I like it a lot. His hand comes to rest at the top of my bra, and he toys with it, lightly running the fabric between his big fingers.

I wet my mouth, my throat so dry you'd think I was lost in the Sahara, but no, right now, I'm just a little lost in Callan.

I widen my fingers, and move them over his flesh, going lower to examine the hard muscles of his abdomen. "Hmm, nice," I say and an adorable smile that turns me a little inside out pulls up the corners of his kissable mouth.

"I think I'm the one who's supposed to be saying it's nice. But I like that you're enjoying touching me, too."

I grin. "So you're saying you like this, then?" I ask, as I take pleasure in all his hills and valleys.

"Oh yeah."

"Good."

My hand stills, indicating it's his turn and he chuckles lightly. He trails his finger lower, dragging it between my breasts and before I even realize what I'm doing, I arch upward, my nipples hardening, aching for attention.

"I like that," I say.

"Me too," he murmurs, his gaze latched on my breasts.

I move my hand. Is he completely naked next to me, or does he sleep in his boxers? I guess I'm about to find out. I inch downward, but my fingers stop when an elastic band prohibits any further exploration. I linger around the band and just lightly brush my fingers over his stomach.

"Fuck," he murmurs, and he slides one big palm over my breasts, taking me into his hand. He massages gently, and lightly rubs his thumb over my aching bud.

"Yes," I hiss, and his breathing changes, becomes a little heavier.

I want to touch him as much as I want him to touch me. With a new kind of want zinging through me, I slide my hand into his boxers, and wrap my palm around his big cock and give him a squeeze.

"Jesus, Gemma," he says with a rough breath.

"You like that, Callan?"

"Yeah, I do."

"I like it too," I say.

His hand slides around my back, and he unhooks my bra to free my breasts. "I'm wondering about something," he says, and I stiffen. Is he having second thoughts? If he is, his brain is telling him one thing, but the cock my hand is wrapped around is telling an entirely different story.

"What's that?" I ask.

"Would you mind if I used something else to touch you?"

"Such as?"

"I was thinking I could use my mouth." He gently squeezes my nipple and my sex clenches. "Right here, specifically," he says. My pulse jumps in anticipation, giving me away. "I'm wondering if you'd like that."

"I guess we won't know until you try," I say, and take in his hungry grin as his head dips. I sink into my pillow as his hot mouth closes around my nipple and with one hand on his cock, lightly pumping up and down, I slide the other hand around his head, letting him know in no uncertain terms how much I love what he's doing. His tongue swirls over my bud, and the way he's touching me, like my pleasure is paramount, warms me from the inside out. This...right here...is how I've always wanted to be touched, but with my ex, sex was for his pleasure, hard and fast and almost...violent.

"Callan," I moan, and he moves to the other breast, giving it the same amount of blissful attention. He spends a long time on my flesh and my lips tingle, wanting to kiss him, to taste him on my tongue.

His head lifts and he shifts. My hand slides from his boxers as he settles himself on top of me. His big palm smooths my hair back from my forehead and intense blue eyes lock on mine.

"Do you know what we're doing here, Gemma?" he asks, his gaze roaming my face, worry mingling with arousal.

"I think we do," I say, to put him at ease. "Two friends just being there for each other. It's nothing more than that."

"I don't have any more to give," he says. "I don't want to hurt you or let you think there could be more."

My heart squeezes for all this man has lost. "I love how honest you are, Callan." I put my hand on his cheek, and his warmth wraps around me like a favorite blanket. "I want to be with you tonight. Like this. It just feels right, don't you think?"

"Yeah, but I shouldn't..." A pained look rips across his face as he briefly looks away. "I shouldn't want. I don't des—"

His words fall off, so I say, "I'm afraid to be with anyone."

"You're not afraid of me, though."

"No, never, but it's okay, Callan. We don't have to."

There's hunger back in his eyes when they lift to mine. "I want to be with you, and it does feel right, Gemma."

"We're just giving each other what we need tonight. No tomorrows." I part my lips in invitation as he nods.

"I'm going to kiss you now. Do you think you'd like that?" he asks, his playfulness back.

I slide my hands around his head. "No," I say, and he stills. "I think I'd love that." His low moan reverberates around us as he closes his mouth over mine. His lips are soft, gentle at first, a slow introduction to let me get used to the feel. I moan and slide my tongue into his mouth to find his and a deep growl rips from his throat. My heart speeds up. I like that I can do that to him, that he chose me to trust, just like I chose him.

He kisses me with hunger, passion, a man starved of a woman's touch for so long, and it makes me want to give him everything he's lacking. I widen my legs, my knees up in the air as his hard cock presses against my center.

"I like everything about this," I murmur when he breaks the kiss. He presses hot, open mouthed kisses to my cheek, sliding lower to bury his face in the hollow of my neck. I might not have seen this man in a while, but the intimacy between us, the honesty and trust is unlike anything I've ever before experienced. How is it possible that I feel so close to this man, so fast?

I'm not sure, but I'm going to revel in it, let it fill the hole in my soul, until past hurts are just that...hurts from the past. He slides down my body, his teeth nipping at the lace on my underwear.

"I'm a little disappointed," he says, and my heart stops beating, until I catch the smirk on his face.

"Oh?"

"I love you in these sexy little panties, but I was hoping to see my clothes on you."

"You were?"

"Yeah, I don't know why? Strange, huh?" he says and slips a finger into the band, running his big rough finger back and forth, back and forth, and I almost cry out, yell at him to touch my clit like that, but I don't want to rush things. I want to take tonight slow, and savor the sweetness in each moment.

"If you like I could get up and get dressed for you." I pretend to move and his growl stops me. I stifle a chuckle.

"Now let's not go crazy," he teases.

"You'll be happy to know I'm not disappointed."

"Glad to hear it."

"I have no desire to see you in my clothes."

His laughter vibrates me, and I sink deeper into the mattress as it strokes my body. I honestly don't ever remember laughing during sex, ever drawing it out with fun, sexy banter. A girl could get used to this kind of sex.

"I promise you won't have to worry about that. Not that there is anything wrong with it, but it's just not my thing."

"You're saying I won't find you in my panties, then," I tease.

"Well, I don't know if I'd go so far as to say that." A thrill goes through me as he dips his fingers into my panties. He parts me with his fingers and lightly strokes my clit. I moan.

"I like your version of being in my panties better," I say.

"Glad you like it." He runs his finger along the length of me. "I like it too."

"Yeah," is all I manage to get out as my thoughts trail off, unable to focus on anything but the pleasure in his touch.

"Want to know what I'd like more?"

"Yes," I say and lift my head to see him. His eyes are completely focused on my panties. "Tell me. No, wait?"

"Wait?"

"Don't tell me, show me."

He exhales. "I was hoping you'd say that." He nips at my panties again, dragging them lower on my hips, just enough to expose my damp sex. "You are so damn wet for me," he says.

"Please touch me," I say, and shock myself. I'm not a girl to open up and ask for things during sex, but with Callan, it's different. This safe space he's created for me has allowed me to relax.

"I'm going to touch you, Gemma. I'm going to do whatever you want me to do."

"I like that. Here's the thing, though. There's something I'm wondering about, too."

He brushes his thumb over my clit and my eyes roll back as I let loose a moan. I love the freedom to just be myself. I try to widen my legs, but my panties prevent it.

"What's that?"

"I was wondering if you'd like it if I put your cock in my mouth?"

"Jesus, Gemma," he growls. "Fuck yeah, I'd like that. But first, this sweet pussy needs my tongue."

"Oh, yes, you're right. It does."

He chuckles against my belly, and lowers his mouth until his tongue is on my clit. I cry out and lift my hips from the bed, grinding against his face, completely shameless in my needs. He swirls his tongue, then flattens it, and presses it against me.

"My God," I cry out, and go up on my elbows to watch him. The deep sound in his throat is a good indication that he likes what he's doing. My sex clenches when he slides one thick finger inside me, and his head lifts to gauge my reaction. My heart tumbles a little, appreciating the check-in. "Yes," I say, and he moves his finger in and out of me as he closes his mouth around my clit and sucks on it, hard. "Callan," I cry. "Yes, like that."

His finger works a miracle inside me, touching me in

places no man has ever touched before, and before I even know what's happening, heat rushes through me, all pleasure centered on the hot spot between my legs, and I let go. Completely. Liquid pleasure pours out of me, and he releases his hold on my clit to lap at me.

"Jesus," he murmurs, and my throat is so tight with happiness, that he likes what he's doing to me, I can barely speak. "I love the taste of you," he murmurs, and continues to lap at me with the soft blade of his tongue.

When I can finally find my voice again, I say, "I bet I'd love the taste of you, too."

His head lifts, his eyes raging with hunger when they latch on mine. "You want to find out?"

"Yeah."

5

CALLAN

With her panties around her thighs—looking so goddamn sexy—I go back on my knees. I pet her lightly until her body stops spasming. Cheeks hot and flushed, she shifts on the bed, and reaches for me with greedy hands. I let her catch me and she tugs me toward her. A sly grin on her face, she gives a playful push until I'm flat on my back. Want dances in her eyes as her gaze slides lower over my body, the visual caress like a soft stroke to my cock. It throbs, grows another inch and tents my boxers.

"You want to see me in your clothes huh?" she teases.

"Right now, I just want to see you in my boxers."

She laughs at that, and presses her small hand over my aching cock, squeezing me through the dark fabric. I groan, and put my hand over hers, lifting my hips and pushing a little harder. She grins, and pushes my hand away, wanting to take things at her speed. She slides her panties off, shimmies on the bed until she's between my legs and grips the elastic band on my boxers. One quick tug frees my cock, and it slaps against my stomach. She takes me into her hands, admiration all over her face as she examines me, long thorough strokes as she weighs me in her palm.

"Nice," she says.

"Yeah," I agree as the warmth of her hands zaps my balls. She runs her hand up and down the length of me, and pre-cum spills from my tip. Fuck, when was the last time I felt like a hormonal teen, ready to explode on contact?

"You do like this," she says, a playful smile turning up the corners of those kissable lips. She puts one leg over mine, and she straddles my leg as she bends forward and runs her soft pink tongue over my crown.

"Fuck yeah," I say.

"Mmm," she moans and lifts her head. "I do like the taste of you."

My cock jumps as she trails her finger down the long length of me. I want her mouth on me, I want it on me so goddamn bad it's all I can do not to take her head and guide her down. But I want to do things on her terms, even if it fucking kills me.

"Let's see what else you like," she says, and closes her mouth around my crown. She leans forward and I grip the bedding as I slide to the back of her throat. She chokes a bit, and I try to pull out, but she's not having any of that. I look down at her, take pleasure in the way I slide in and out of her hot mouth, but as I watch her, I get the sense that this is about her as much as it's about me. She's experimenting, having sex her way, the way she wants, and goddammit, I'm going to give her that—and I'm not going to hate it. Nope, I'm going to fucking explode down her throat as she figures out what she likes in bed. What a hardship, huh?

She moans around my throbbing cock, and the tremors race through my body. She is so good at this. I plop from her mouth, and she uses her tongue, runs it over my tight skin. Her exploration is slow, thorough, completely effective in taking me to the damn edge, and leaving me hovering there. I want to be inside her when I come, but this, how can I say no to head when it's this fucking good for both of us?

"Gemma. I'm really close. Tell me what you want. Do you want me to come in your mouth, or do you want me inside you?"

She frowns like she's struggling with the answer, and I like that she wants to try everything with me. She runs her fingers up and down my cock, and I clench down on my teeth to hold on.

"What if I wanted both?"

She cups my balls and in that instant, I know I'm fucked. I also know it won't take me long to be hard again. It's been way too fucking long since I've had a soft warm body in my bed, a mouth or hand on me.

"You can have both," I say, through gritted teeth.

"Good." Smiling she takes me back into her mouth, and I go so deep, I'm practically down her throat. She sucks, her hot mouth squeezing around me, pulling my orgasm.

"I'm there," I say, and grip her hair, tugging it to the side so I can watch myself spurt into her throat. She keeps those lips tightly wrapped around me as I let go, pour my release into the depths of her throat. She drinks me in, her gulping sounds fucking me over in ways that make me hard again. She stays between my legs, and my cock jerks with the final release.

Grinning, she eases off me and my cock flops to my stomach. She lightly strokes me. "That was nice," she says. "I liked it."

I laugh. I don't know why, but a laugh bubbles from my throat, and her grin widens. "Yeah, I like that too."

"It was..." She narrows her eyes like she's trying to find the right word.

"Fun," I say, helping her out.

She nods. "Yeah, it was fun." Her gaze moves over my face. "You good, Callan?"

"I'm good," I say even though I'm not sure I am. It's been so long since I've been with anyone, and I'm not even sure I deserve happiness. "You good, Gemma?"

She nods and I sit up to put my hand on the side of her face, my heart thumping. Fuck, man, I'd like to spend five minutes with the asshole who never treated her properly. "Sex can be anything you want, Gemma. Anything."

"We can have more, right?" Big eager eyes blink up at me.

"Of course. But first let me go get you a glass of water, and I'm going to need just a minute."

"A whole minute," she teases. "Right, right, I forgot, you're a dad now. The stamina from your younger years is gone."

"Like hell it is," I say, and poke my finger into my chest. "And this dad is going to fuck you right. Tomorrow, you won't be able to walk, and you won't be able to wipe the bliss off your face. Everyone who looks at you will know you're a well taken care of woman."

Her eyes glaze. "I want that."

"You want me, Gemma?" I ask, and while I know she does, for some strange reason I need to hear her say it. I've been so closed off, hiding away in my house with my daughter, away from civilization for the most part...I guess other than my daughter I've not felt needed or wanted. It never bothered me before. Why it does now is a mystery.

"I want you, Callan," she says, and snuggles down into a pillow, spreading her legs in invitation. "I believe your minute is up."

I laugh as I pull up my boxers and dart downstairs to the kitchen. I pour a glass of water, drink the whole thing and refill the glass. Back in the room, Gemma is still sprawled on the bed, waiting for me. Man, I forgot how much fun sex—

with a partner—was. I'm just glad we're on the same page here. Neither one of us are looking for more.

"That took forever," she says.

"Sorry about that," I say and cross the room, settling beside her on the mattress. She takes a big drink and wipes her mouth with the back of her hand. I take in her flushed cheeks. I've never seen her look more beautiful. I can only imagine how she's going to look after I've been inside her, with her orgasming around my cock.

My heart thumps a little faster, my dick rising to the occasion when she licks a bead of water from her bottom lip. I growl, and push her mess of hair from her face.

"You're beautiful," I say.

"Thanks," she says. "I haven't felt beautiful in a long time." I frown at her. "You make me feel good about myself, though."

"I'm glad."

"Just for the record," she says and puts her hand on my chest. "You're not so bad yourself. Climbing that big ladder does wonders for these abs."

I grin. "Thanks, babe."

Her fingers trail over my flesh, tickling me, and my stomach clenches. "Speaking of climbing," she says with a crook of her finger.

"You want me to climb on, Gemma?" I ask, loving the way this woman wants me. No mind games, no playing hard to get. She just straight up wants my cock, and isn't afraid to admit it. Damned if I don't like that.

"Yes please," she says and slides one finger between her breasts, going lower and lower until she's touching herself. Jesus. This woman is all kinds of surprises and all kinds of sexy. How a man couldn't treat her right is beyond me, but I plan to make up for all her bad experiences tonight. I take her water glass, set it on the nightstand, and climb over her body.

My cock is rock hard by the time my mouth finds hers for a deep, thorough kiss. The only look I want on this woman when she wakes tomorrow is ecstasy, not fear of facing her ex.

I smooth her hair back, and take in her eyes. My heart misses a beat. This woman trusts me, and while I want that, for a brief second it scares the shit out of me. My wife trusted me too, and I couldn't save her. But those dark thoughts are for another time.

"Condom," I murmur as her hips lift, her body beckoning my cock.

"Please tell me you have some."

"I do." I reach into my nightstand, and pull out a foil package. "They've been in there a while." I try to see if it has an expiry date, but don't get the chance before Gemma's eager hands are taking it from me.

"I want to put it on you."

"Okay," I tear off my boxers and go to my knees. She sits up, shimmies back a bit and tears into the foil. There's almost a fascinated look on her face as she examines the condom. "You've never done this before have you?"

"No, and I always read about it in my romance books. Usually the guy is all hard and the girl fumbles and he nearly comes."

"That's pretty much it," I say, and she chuckles.

She presses the condom to my crown, and I groan as her warm hands run it down the length of me.

"That wasn't so hard," she says.

"You don't think," I say and take my cock into my hand. "Seems pretty hard to me."

She laughs, and it filters through me, filling my soul in a way it hasn't been filled in years. Tonight, here with Gemma, it's good for both of us. She falls back onto the bed, her body wide open and welcoming me.

"I can't wait to feel you inside me," she says.

"You know, I know things in the bedroom haven't been great for you, but you sure do know the right things to say to drive a man crazy."

Her eyes light up. She clearly likes that. "I like driving you crazy, Callan. Being with you makes me forget about the real world for a while."

"Me too," I say, and rub my thumb over her clit. She inhales deeply, and her head rolls to the side.

"I love the way you touch me." She zeroes back in on me. "I'm so glad you banged into me."

"I'm about to do it again," I say with a grin, and a smile splits her face when she gets the joke.

"Bang into me, Callan."

I fall over her and my cock probes her opening. I grab my dick, run circles around her clit until her head is rolling from side to side, her body delirious with want. "You like that, Gemma? You like when I tease this sexy body of yours with the tip of my cock?"

"Yes," she breathes out, "More."

I press against her opening, and glide into her, seating myself high and going still. "Is this what you want?"

"It's exactly what I want," she says. "It's exactly what I need."

"It's what I need too," I admit, and move my hips, slow at first, giving her time to get used to my girth and the fullness, but also to ease her into this, and give her as much pleasure as possible.

"Callan," she says and runs her nails along my back, tugging me tighter against her body. Her hard nipples score my chest as we come together as one, each pushing and pulling, each giving and taking, the way good sex should be. I find her mouth again, kiss her and tangle my tongue with hers. Jesus, she's so open and welcoming and responsive to every little touch.

My cock is so damn hard it wants release, but I hang on. No way am I going to come before her. I bury my mouth in the hollow of her throat, and shift so I can tease her nipple between my fingers. I brush it lightly, give it a little pinch that produces the telltale yelp that lets me know she likes what I'm doing. I love discovering her body, finding out her likes.

"You feel so good," she says, her knees coming up to hug my sides. The position opens her more, and allows me to go deeper. I pull almost all the way out, and glide back in again, yet can't seem to get deep enough.

She grows wetter, and I reach between our bodies to play with her swollen clit. I stroke her and her mouth opens, no sound escaping as her sex muscles clench around me.

"My God," I say as she comes all over my cock, her hot juices burning my flesh and soaking my balls. They tighten, eager for release, but I want to hang on, enjoy each pulse as she rides out the wave.

She pants and curls forward, a full body tremor racing through her, and she—goddammit, she's never looked more beautiful. "That's it, come all over my cock," I say. Her spasms finally settle, and she pulls my mouth to hers. Her kisses are softer now, less hurried, as I piston into her, chasing my own orgasm now.

"Yes, just like that," she says, her words encouraging me on. I pull out and slide back in, a fast, blunt stroke that sheds the last of my restraint. I give in to the pleasure and pour into her. "I feel you," she says, her arms around me holding me tight as I deplete myself.

Breathing hard, I collapse on top of her. "Jesus, Gemma. That was..."

"Fun," she says, and I lift my head to see her.

"Yeah, fun."

"Like a lot of fun."

"Yeah."

"Like so fun, we should probably do it again."

I laugh and roll to the side to discard the condom. "Yeah, but you're going to have to give me a minute. Maybe two this time."

She grins at me, and wets her lips. "I've got time." She gives a lazy, catlike stretch. "I don't have to be anywhere until tomorrow." My heart squeezes in the oddest way at the thoughts of her leaving my bed, of not seeing her again for another few years.

I touch her body, run my hand down her stomach. "Still burning up?"

"Uh huh," she murmurs. "Mr. Sexy Firefighter lit a fuse inside me." She reaches down and squeezes my cock. "And the only thing that will extinguish it is this big hose."

I laugh at that. "What have I created?"

"In T-minus two minutes, you're going to find out."

6

GEMMA

My lids slowly open, catch the splash of sunshine slanting in on the wall. For a second I don't know where I am, but with the way my body is feeling, so gloriously sated, I could be in a ditch somewhere and wouldn't care. A little sigh escapes my lips as heated memories fill me. I roll and find the other side of the bed empty. A burst of unease moves through me, and my eyes open bigger. All worry evaporates when I find a very sexy firefighter leaning against the doorjamb with a cup of coffee in his hand.

"Is that for me?" I ask and sit up a bit. The blankets roll from my naked body and I pull them back up.

He pulls himself up to his full height and I resist the urge to drool as I take pleasure in the sight of him. This morning he's dressed in a navy T-shirt and jeans that hang low on his hips. I used to notice Callan before, but he was taken, so I kept my eyes to myself. Now, though, he might not be looking for a relationship—neither am I—but I can look my fill, and look I will.

"Could be."

I arch a brow and push my hair from my shoulders. "Could be?

"Depends on what you'd do for it."

"Well, that sounds like a challenge to me."

His sexy grin turns me inside out, and when I hear a noise from downstairs, I stiffen.

"Shoot, Kaitlyn will know I slept over."

"It's okay. I explained that it was late, and she's fine. It's not the first time I've had a sleepover."

I angle my head. Last night he told me he hasn't been with anyone since Zoe. "Oh?"

"Yeah, sometimes the nanny stays when I work nights, and sometimes the other female firefighters and wives of the male ones stay over."

"You have a whole harem."

That pulls a laugh from him. He holds his empty hand up, palm out. "All platonic."

He comes toward me and I stare at his hard body as mine quivers in awareness. God, what we did last night. It was so incredible. The way he made me feel, both physically and emotionally.

"It really is nice that you have such a great support system."

"It is."

He hands me the cup but before I can take it, he pulls it back. "Wait, what are you willing to do for this?

I crook my finger, and he leans into me. "Well, if we were alone, I'd be willing to go on my knees and take your cock into my mouth." I love the tortured groan that follows. "But since we're not, I guess all I can do is give you a thank you."

"Great, now I have a hard-on," he says, as he hands me the cup and I take a much-needed sip of coffee.

He sits beside me and the bed dips. I smile at him, and my heart is so damn full. He smiles back, and I love this. I love everything about this morning after. No awkwardness. No expectations. We both know where each other stands. I could get used to an arrangement like this.

"How are you feeling?" he asks, and like it's the most natural thing in the world to do, he brushes my hair from my face and tucks it behind my ear. The tenderness in his caress is like a soft hug to all the hurts inside me.

"Amazing," I say. "How about you. You good?"

He rakes his hands through his hair, and gives a low slow whistle. "Gemma, last night was everything I needed."

"Good. It was what I needed too." I steal a glance at the clock and my heart sinks. "And now I need to get going to the Cape."

"Right. Do you mind coming with me to drop Kaitlyn off to her grandparents?"

"Actually, I haven't seen your parents in years, Callan. I'd love to say hello."

His smile is filled with warmth and appreciation. "They'd love that too."

He leans into me, and places a soft kiss on my lips. From the look on his face when he pulls back, he's as surprised by it as I am. He shakes his head. "You want to jump in the shower?"

"Yeah, if you don't mind."

"Go for it. I'll have breakfast ready for you."

"That's very nice, but you don't have to go to the trouble."

"After all the trouble you went through for me last night," he teases. "It's the least I could do."

"It wasn't a hardship, Callan," I say, and tug the sheet from the bed to wrap around myself. "Where the heck are my clothes?" I scan the floor.

"On the dresser." I follow the direction he's pointing. "I picked them up earlier and folded them."

"Such a domestic dad," I say.

He slaps my ass. "So saucy. Now go."

I snatch up my clothes and hurry to the shower. Since I have no supplies with me, I use his soap. As I lather, it brings a smile back to my face. For the rest of the day, I'm going to smell like him. Hey, maybe that will go a long way with Brad. If he smells another man's soap on my skin, maybe it will prove to him that I've moved on and seriously have no intention of getting back together with him. I rinse off, and climb into yesterday's clothes. A chuckle catches in my throat. Back in college I never once did the walk of shame, yet here I am doing it with Callan, no less.

I head downstairs, and Kaitlyn lifts her head from her coloring book. "Miss Davis," she says. "Can we play the piano again?"

I relax. I wasn't sure if this was going to be awkward or not. I'm about to answer, when Callan comes into the room, my coffee refreshed. "We don't have time today, kiddo. We all have places to be," he says. "But, if Miss Davis can fit you in to her schedule, we can set up some lessons over the summer."

"Really, Daddy!" she squeals and jumps up and down. "Yay!"

"One thing," I say. "How about when we're at home you call me Gemma."

She shrugs. "Okay. When can we start, Gemma?"

"I'm going to be away this weekend. How about I look at my schedule and we'll plan for when you get back from your grandparents."

"That's when I'm getting Gilbert. Maybe you could come and help us pick him out."

I hesitate for a second and Callan rolls a shoulder, leaving it up to me. "We'll see," I say.

"Kaitlyn, go brush your teeth and finish your packing.

We're leaving shortly." Callan's knuckles brush mine, and he nods toward the kitchen. "Breakfast is ready."

Delicious smells reach my nose and my stomach grumbles. My breakfast usually consists of coffee and toast, but after building up an appetite last night, I'm game for something meatier. "If it's anything like your pizza last night, I'd say I'm in for a treat."

I follow him to the kitchen and lower myself into a chair and he puts a box of cereal in front of me. My jaw falls, and Callan laughs.

"Chocolate Puffs, breakfast of champions."

I shake my head at him, but I totally love how funny he is. He's not had it easy, but he's so easy to be around.

"I'll stick to coffee, thanks."

He takes the box away and sets a plate with scrambled eggs, sausage, and toast in front of me."

My stomach grumbles louder. "Now this is what I'm talking about," I say and pick up my fork. I dig in and moan as the flavors hit my tongue. "This is delicious."

"I aim to please."

I grin at him. "Consider me pleased." He sits beside me. "Did you already eat?"

"I ate with Kaitlyn."

I frown. "Sorry I slept in."

"Don't be. It's Saturday."

"Next time, I'll cook for you." As soon as the words leave my mouth, I shake my head. "I don't know why I said that."

He opens his mouth, about to answer, but Kaitlyn comes into the room. "I can't find my pink bathing suit."

"I'll help you." He pushes to his feet, and I go back to finishing the food on my plate. They both appear back in the kitchen by the time I'm done. I rinse my dish and set it in the open dishwasher.

"All set," I say and pick up my purse. "Wait, what did I do with my phone?"

"I think I saw it on the coffee table. You were on it last night when I came downstairs after tucking Kaitlyn in."

"I only lose it about ten times a day."

I find it on the coffee table, and cringe when I see all the texts from Brad.

"Everything okay?" Callan asks.

"Yup," I say and five minutes later, we're piling back into the car, and I note the suitcase and duffle bag Callan is putting in the trunk. Kaitlyn sure packs heavily for her grand-parents' place. In the back seat, Kaitlyn plays on her children's iPad, and I sing along quietly to the song on the radio.

"You have a really nice voice. I never knew that."

"Thanks. Singing lessons when I was young."

Warm contentment settles in my stomach as I take in Callan's profile. It's going to be hard going to his place once a week to give Kaitlyn lessons, and keeping my hands to myself. He awakened my body in glorious ways last night, ways unlike any other man. That thought fills my stomach with dread. Dammit, I want to go to my parents, but on the other hand I'm really sick about it. Maybe I'll get lucky and Brad will be on shift. It's wishful thinking.

"Something on your mind?" Callan asks, when he turns to find me staring at my lap.

"No, I'm good," I say and force a smile.

"Yeah, I hope you don't play poker."

"I'm that easy to read?"

He reaches across the seat, takes my hand into his and gives it a little squeeze. "It's going to be fine, I promise."

I nod, even though I know it's not going to be fine or something he can promise. I'm not even sure why he's saying that to me. I guess he's just being kind and supportive. I go quiet, and Kaitlyn perks up when we pull into his parents' driveway. I smile. I have fond memories of hanging at this house when we were in high school.

The front door opens and out walks Mr. and Mrs. Ward. Kaitlyn unbuckles, jumps from her seat and dashes up the steps for a hug. My heart swells.

"That's sweet," I say.

"Yeah, it is. Kaitlyn is the best thing that ever happened to me."

I angle my head and take in the love shining in his eyes as he gazes at his daughter. "Do you think you'd ever have more?"

The words are barely out of my mouth before he's giving me a fast, "No."

"Okay," I say, the look on his face tearing at my heart. He loved and lost and he's so goddamn frightened to lose again, he won't even try. A guy like him deserves a good woman in his life, in his daughter's life. "I'm sorry, that was none of my business."

"I don't mind you asking. You can ask me whatever you want. It's just that more kids aren't in the cards for me. What about you, Gemma? Do you want kids? Is it okay if I ask that?"

"You can, and yes, I've always wanted a big family. I'm just not interested in a relationship right now. I need time for myself, time to just heal emotionally, and I have a hard time trusting. It's going to be a long time before I open myself up to anyone again. I might not ever, but I guess it's the twenty-first century and I don't really need a man in my life to have a child, right?"

"You're right, you don't." His fingers lightly graze my arm. "But you opened yourself up to me," he says, as he rakes his teeth over his bottom lip, his gaze going to my mouth.

A hard quiver goes through me. "Yeah, but that's different." I glance up to see Mrs. Ward still on the deck, waiting for us, while Kaitlyn drags her grandfather inside.

"I know. But I'm glad we went for it." He squeezes my hand again. "Come on. Let's go say hello."

I open my door and step from the car. Callan grabs the suitcase from the trunk, and we walk to the steps together. At first Callan's mother seems shocked that there is a woman with their son, but after she realizes who I am, she pulls me in for a hug.

"It's so good to see you, Gemma," Blue eyes the color of her son's glisten with happiness. "It's been too long."

"It's good to see you too, Mrs. Ward."

She gives a little wave. "Oh, call us Colleen and Roger," she says.

I smile and she waves her hand toward the door. "Can you guys come in for a coffee, get caught up?"

"I actually can't," I say, and crinkle up my nose because I'd love to spend more time here. "I'm on my way to the Cape for a family reunion."

"How lovely, another time then."

"That'd be great."

Callan gives his mother a kiss on the cheek. "I'll check in with you guys tonight. If you have any trouble, just call."

"Don't worry about us, we're fine. You two go on and have some fun."

I open my mouth about to tell her it's just me going to the Cape, but Kaitlyn comes running back onto the deck to drag her grandmother inside.

We head back to the car, and I take in Callan's profile again as he backs from the driveway. "What street are you on?" he asks.

"Major, just two streets over from the school."

I hum along to the song as he negotiates the busy Saturday afternoon traffic, and when he pulls up in front of my townhouse, I reach for the handle. "Thanks so much, Callan." I hesitate for a second. "When I get back from the weekend, we can discuss Kaitlyn's lessons."

He nods. "Or we can discuss them on the weekend."

"What?"

He taps the steering wheel. "We can discuss them over the weekend because I'm coming to the family gathering with you."

My head rears back and I bump it on the window. "Ow," I rub my head, sure I've heard him wrong. Yeah, I might have thought about it, but I wouldn't go so far as to ask him. That's crossing the friendship line. Then again, we kind of did that already last night in bed.

"Are you okay?" he asks.

"Yeah, just a bump, and I think I heard you wrong. You said you were coming with me?"

He scrubs his face, and he nods. "Yup, I am."

"You can't just...come."

"Why not. I'm on my days off, and I already packed a bag. Hurry on in and get your stuff so we can get going. We don't want to keep everyone waiting."

"Callan, I need to change my clothes, get packed—"

He turns to me and takes my hand. "If you're going to be long, I'll come in and help. But if you think I'm going to let you do this weekend alone, when your douche-bag ex is going to be there, to intimidate you, or whatever else he might have planned to win you back, then you don't know me at all."

My heart turns over in my chest, as tears pound behind my eyes. I honestly can't believe he's suggesting this. I wouldn't in a million years ask, even though having him by my side would certainly send a message, and...I also really like hanging out with him.

I glance down and twist my shirt in my hands. "I can't ask you to do that."

"You're not asking. Now go get your stuff."

I take a deep breath. Am I really going to let him get involved in my troubles? Although, judging by the stubborn set of his jaw, I'm not sure I have a choice.

I open my mouth and close it again, and a moan crawls out of his throat. "Are we about to have our first argument as a couple?"

I grin at that, a warm but weird sensation taking up residence in my stomach as I consider that. "No, we're not. I'll get my stuff." I reach for the door and turn back to him. "Thanks, Callan."

"You bet."

CALLAN

The closer we get to her parents' house, the more agitated Gemma becomes. I reach across the seat and take her hand. "You okay?"

She nods. "I'm actually looking forward to seeing my folks and my sisters. Do you remember Amanda and Nicole?"

"I remember Amanda the most. She was the funny one. Always carrying on and cracking jokes."

"Funny one? The annoying one, you mean." She rolls her eyes. "She always liked to embarrass me. Still does. She'll probably do the same to you."

"Oh yeah."

She purses her lips. "Although, she never really tormented Brad."

"Maybe it's just a big sister thing."

She shrugs. "I guess."

"Did she like Brad?"

"To be honest, she never really said one way or the other." She frowns, and glances down. "Come to think of it, they never really interacted very much when we're all together."

"Maybe he couldn't pull the wool over her eyes."

"It's possible. She's never said anything to me. Well, that's not exactly true. After we broke up, she told me..." Her words fall off and she bites her bottom lip.

"What?"

"She told me..." She cups her face.

"What?" I ask and laugh.

"She told me to hook up with some random hot guy and fuck Brad right out of my mind."

I laugh at that. "I'm glad you took her advice."

She laughs with me. "You're not random, Callan."

"But you're saying I'm hot though, right?"

"My God, are you twelve?" she asks, but she's laughing so hard tears are in her eyes. The tension in my shoulders ebb away. I like that I can distract her like this.

"Maybe your sister only teases people she likes," I say.

"Yeah, maybe. I guess we hope she embarrasses you then."

"Well that's something to look forward to I guess."

"Both my sisters became teachers, too."

"Like your mom."

"You remember?"

I nod. "Do you spend much time with them?"

"Not as much as I'd like. We were all pretty close growing up, though."

"Only child here."

"Did you want siblings?"

"Yeah, I actually did." I'm sure Kaitlyn would love to have siblings, but that's just not in the cards for us. I stare at the road; cars pass in a blur. Am I depriving my daughter of a fulfilled childhood by closing myself off to the idea of a family and more children? Shit, I guess I never thought about that before.

"I think it's my turn to ask if you're okay?" Gemma says, dragging my focus back.

I scratch my chin. "Yeah, sorry. I zoned out there for a second."

"Want to talk about it?"

I shrug. "Just wondering if I'm doing right by my daughter, you know."

She puts her hand on my legs. "You are. You grew up without siblings," she says, smart enough to know where my thoughts have gone. "You turned out all right."

I grin. "You say that now. Wait until after you spend the weekend with me. You're going to see all kinds of crazy."

She laughs, and it lightens my mood. "I'm sure I'll still like you, Callan. Wait, weren't you voted most likeable in our yearbook?"

"I was able to hide the crazy. What were you voted?" I ask and cast her a glance.

She chuckles. "Most likely to end up on Broadway. Probably because of my music and dancing."

"That's right, you were in all the school plays." I nod and relax into my seat. "I forgot about that. I forgot that look on your face when you used to dance."

"You remember that?"

"Yeah, you were so happy. Dancing was an outlet for you, wasn't it?"

"It was."

"Like you could be free." She nods. "You've sort of lost that, Gemma." Her body tightens, and she looks away. "It's okay," I say. "You can tell me."

"I haven't felt free in a long time."

My stomach coils. Her ex had taken a lot from her and dammit, if I don't want to give it back. "Maybe you can dance for me sometime."

"I take it you mean privately," she says and whacks my stomach.

I grab her hand. "Of course, I mean privately and preferably with a pole," I say to lighten the mood. But it doesn't change the fact that I want happiness and the euphoria that comes from dancing back in her life. "How is it you always know what I'm thinking?"

"You're a guy," she states, and I laugh out loud.

"That I am."

"But you're a good guy, Callan. I need that in my life right now."

"Yeah, you do," I say.

"Just up left here. The one with the triple garage."

"Every house has a triple garage," I say. The homes here are gorgeous. Gemma takes a big breath and lets it out as I pull into the driveway, which is already filled with cars. I kill the engine, and we step from the car. "Nice place."

"It's gorgeous," she says as I pull our bags from the trunk.

"Wait, I just thought of something. Are your parents going to make us sleep in separate rooms?"

"I'm a grown woman, Callan. Of course not."

I take her hand in mine, and dip my head. "They're not going to like this—us—though, are they? They want you back with Brad?"

"They do, but they always liked you, Callan."

I glance around the big estate, take in the perfectly manicured lawns. "At least we don't have to pretend."

"What do you mean?"

"We're pretty good together."

"Yeah, we are," she says with a smile. "And really, they just want to see me happy." She tries to take her bag from me, but I toss the strap over my shoulder.

"What kind of an impression would I make if I let you carry your own bag?"

"You're kind of an old-fashioned guy, aren't you?" She holds her hand up. "I'm not saying that's a bad thing. I actually like it."

Without thinking, I lean into her and place a soft kiss on her lips. I break it and her fingers go to her mouth, lightly linger there as warmth moves into her cheeks, staining them a pretty shade of pink. "What was that for?"

I'm not really sure, and I probably shouldn't admit that. A movement near the front door catches my attention. "It was for our audience," I say.

Her gaze flies to the front door, and she grabs my arm. "It's Brad," she says through clenched teeth, her body tightening all over again.

"It's okay," I say and take her hand. Presenting a united front, we saunter up the driveway. Brad's dark eyes are pinned on me.

He stands to his full height when we reach the bottom step. "I didn't know you were bringing a friend," he says.

"Brad," Gemma says. "This is Callan Ward. We're friends from high school."

I laugh. "That was then. We're a lot more than that now, babe." I slide my hand around her and drag her close. She smiles up at me and I know we're putting on a performance, but my heart beats just a little faster at the warm gratitude in her eyes.

"You didn't tell me you were seeing someone." Brad squares his shoulders, his anger barely contained. What a fucking asshole to think she owed him any sort of explanation. He's not her keeper. No one is.

I slowly drag my gaze from Gemma. "My fault," I say. "I've been keeping her pretty occupied." Brad glares at me, but I'm not afraid of the motherfucker. If he wants to pick on someone his own size, bring that shit on.

The door opens and a girl with similar features to Gemma comes out. "I thought I heard voices," she says, and pulls Gemma in for a hug. I watch the exchange as Brad watches me, but I don't pay him much attention.

"Amanda, do you remember Callan?"

"Callan Ward, of course." She turns to me and brings me in for a hug. "So nice to see you again, and I'm sorry, we're all huggers," she says with a laugh, but I instantly like her. She steps back and her gaze goes from her sister to me back to her sister. "Wait, are you two..."

I pull Gemma back in. "Yeah, we are," I say.

She gives us a big grin. "You two make the cutest couple. I always knew you would."

"What are you talking about, Amanda?"

"Oh, come on, Gemma. Don't pretend you didn't have a crush on him in high school. He had the nicest body." She gives me a once over. "From the looks of things, he still does."

"Yeah, he does," Gemma says, dreamily.

I grin. "Thanks, babe."

She frowns as she turns to her sister. "But seriously, why do you say stuff like that? Just to embarrass us?"

"I'm your big sister, it's what big sisters do, and you, my little sister, have some explaining to do. Clearly there are some things you forgot to tell me the last time we talked." She puts her arm around Gemma and drags her from me.

"I'm sure David wouldn't like you commenting on another man's ass," Gemma says.

"David knows what he got himself into when he asked me to marry him, Gemma." Amanda leads her sister into the house, completely ignoring Brad. Seems to me Gemma isn't the only one who isn't a fan of her ex. I like her sister even more. I take the steps, and Brad stands in front of me, blocking my path.

"Where do you think you're going?" he asks.

I lift the bag in my hand. "To Gemma's room. Drop our things off and then to hang out. If you wouldn't mind moving." I keep my temper in check. Man, I've come across assholes like this in my career before. Guys that can't take no for an answer, thrive on power and control. Worry for Gemma trickles through me at all the red flags I see in his behavior.

"I do mind."

"Then we're going to have a problem," I say.

He crosses his arms and sticks his chest out. "What I have a problem with is you and Gemma."

"Not much I can do about that." I say.

"We were going to work things out this weekend, try to get back together."

"News to me."

"What the fuck is really going on here? Gemma never told me she was seeing someone."

"What Gemma does is none of your business, maybe that's why she never told you. The only one she has to answer to is herself. Not even to me."

He fists his hands, the veins on his neck bulging.

"We're a couple now, pal," I say. "You'll have to get used to it. Or not. Either way, I don't care."

"I'm not your pal. In fact, I don't much like you," he says.

"Not a problem for me. I already have a best friend." My phone buzzes in my pocket. "That's him messaging me right now." Taking off with Gemma happened so fast, I never had time to text Mason. He's probably wondering where the fuck I am. What would he think if he knew what I was doing? He's been after me to move on, but I'm not sure this is what he would have had in mind. I make a mental note to shoot him a text.

Brad's nostrils flare as we stand there, a pissing contest if I ever saw one. Gemma's mother comes outside, and Brad's demeanor instantly changes. She tucks a strand of blonde hair behind her ear. "Callan," she says. "Gemma told me you were here. So nice to see you again."

Brad smiles at her. "We were just getting to know each other, Janice."

"Well, come on out back, and have a beer. We'd love to hear what you've been up to, Callan."

"Yeah we'd love to hear," Brad says.

We step inside and Gemma's eyes are filled with anxiety when they meet mine.

"Hey babe, want to show me which room is ours?"

"Sure," she says, and I hold my hand out for her. She slides hers into mine and we head upstairs. Once in her room, she shuts the door. "Sorry about leaving you outside like that."

"Not a problem. I can handle that asshole."

"I know you can," she says and steps up to me. She puts her arms around me and rests her head on my chest. "You know what. I really am glad you're here. It was so much easier facing him with you by my side."

I run my hand down her hair and kiss the top of her head. "He's not going to hurt you, Gemma. Not ever again," I say, as a sinking feeling settles in the pit of my stomach. I wasn't able to protect my wife and unborn son. I never got to them in time. What if Gemma found herself in trouble and I wasn't there to protect her? I swallow down the pain rising in me. "We better get out there. I'm going to need a cold one."

She uncoils her hands from around my back. "Amanda was happy we were together."

"I like her."

"She likes you too."

"Let's go work on the rest of them."

We head back down the stairs, and she gives me a quick tour of the place, and we walk out back, the Atlantic Ocean on their doorsteps. "Such a great home," I say, and Gemma's father stands.

"Callan, son, it's so good to see you. How have you been?"

"Things are good, Jim. Good to see you again," I say and smile as he shakes my hand.

"Let me get you a beer and then introduce you to everyone." There are a good twenty people on the wide expanse of deck. Children are running about playing and adults are chatting and putting back drinks. Jim hands me a can of beer, and I crack it as he does the introduction of friends and family, and I work hard to remember all the names.

Brad comes back out onto the deck. I have no idea where he's been. Probably running my name through his database.

I take a seat and Gemma drops down into the chair next to me. "So, what do you do, son?" Jim asks.

"Firefighter," I say.

Janice sets a platter of fresh fruit on the table and I pick up a strawberry and dip it into the Cool Whip. I hand it to Gemma and grab one for myself.

"If my memory serves me correctly," he says, and winks. "Usually it doesn't," he adds and everyone laughs. "But I do remember you saying in high school that you wanted to be a firefighter."

"It's the only thing I ever wanted to do," I say. "And that's a great memory you have."

Someone, and I believe it's Gemma's aunt, pipes in, "Just like Brad. He always wanted to be a police officer."

"That's right, Donna," Brad says. "I'm working my way up to lieutenant."

Donna beams up at him, and I take Gemma's hand into mine. I bring it to my mouth for a kiss as Brad continues to talk about his accomplishments.

I lean into her. "Do you swim down there?" I ask as I take in the long dock and the wharf in the water. I also note the speed boat.

"I haven't for a while," Gemma says. "It's the Atlantic Ocean. It's always freezing. I prefer the pool."

I glance around, and spot the pool off to the side of the house. I hadn't noticed it earlier. "Did you want to go swimming?" Gemma asks.

"I forgot to pack a suit."

"We can head into town and get you one," Gemma says. "They have some great shops."

"Maybe we can have a game of pool volleyball later," Jim says.

"Great idea," Brad says, and I lift my head to see him perched on the deck railing. "Station champion three years running."

"Sounds like fun," I say.

"Do you drive a firetruck?" a small voice asks, and I turn to find a boy about four standing beside me, a toy truck in his hand. "I don't drive it, but I ride in the cab."

"I like firetrucks," the boy says.

Gemma's sister Nicole drops into one of the empty chairs near me. "Caleb loves any vehicle that makes a noise," she says and ruffles his hair. "Don't you, bud?"

Caleb's eyes are big and wide when he says, "Uncle Brad lets me use the sirens in his car."

Uncle Brad?

He's definitely not the boy's uncle, but no one corrects him. He's seriously inserted himself into this family if the kids are calling him uncle. No wonder it was hard for Gemma to get out of the relationship. It might have been easier if she told her parents what was going on, but I get not wanting to cause tension between families.

"I can bring the cruiser by tomorrow, Caleb," Brad says.

"Yay," Caleb hollers and starts making a whirring sound.

"I want to ride in it too," Caleb's cousin, I think her name was Jenna, says.

"Of course." Brad takes a drink from his can. "We can all go for a ride."

"This summer, I'm arranging a tour of the fire station," Gemma says to her nephew as Janice and a few of the women head inside to refresh their drinks and people break off into conversations. Brad, however, still seems very interested in ours. "Maybe you could come?"

"Can I, Mommy? Can I ride in the firetruck?"

"I bet we can arrange that," Nicole answers.

Amanda comes over. "My kidlets will want in on that," she says, a small child on her hip, while the other, around two years old, hugs her legs. She gives me a wink. "Rumor has it firefighters give the best rides?"

"Ohmigod," Gemma says under her breath as I nearly choke on my beer.

"Uh, yeah," I say, and glance around the table, but the only ones listening in are Brad and Nicole.

Amanda pops a strawberry into her mouth. "I heard another rumor too. Something about firefighters having the biggest hoses." My jaw drops, and I have no idea how to respond. She gives a dismissive wave. "Wait, that's not a rumor, Gemma already confirmed that." She leans into me, her words for my ears only. "Sometimes you gotta fight fire with fire."

8

GEMMA

"I can't believe Amanda said that," I say and shake my head as we stroll down Main Street, taking in all the quaint shops, the buildings all painted in bright colors. Off in the distance water beats against the shore and the smell of salt is thick in the air. I'd forgotten how much I love it here.

"She obviously doesn't like Brad."

"I never knew that. She never went out of her way for him, but I guess she wanted to support me, no matter what."

"We don't want to provoke a guy like him, Gemma. But we also can't let him think he has any sort of control over you. I think it's just best if you spend the rest of the weekend close to my side."

I nudge him. "Not a hardship. I like being with you."

"I like being with you, too. I like your whole family, actually." He glances around. "I don't think Brad will fuck with you, as long as he knows you're with me." He frowns. "He sure knows how to fool your family, though. Most of them, anyway."

"Like I said, he wears a different face behind closed doors, and his parents, Misty and John, have been friends with my folks forever. I don't want any trouble, Callan. It's over between us, and I think we drove that point home."

"Good. I'm not much into pissing contests, to be honest." He takes a deep breath, and glances into one of my favorite bookstores, his mood mellowing. "Kaitlyn would love it here."

"We could bring her here sometime," I say, and he nods, like he knows that's never going to happen. Once this weekend is over, we'll go back to being friends, and soon enough, school will start up and we'll rarely cross paths again. I ignore the odd little ache in my stomach at that reminder. "Over there," I say. "They have some great jewelry. Let's get her something."

"Yeah?"

"Of course."

He scratches his face as we cross the street. "I have a confession." I eye him. "I have no idea how to pick out jewelry for a six-year-old."

"Good thing you've got me, then."

"Yeah, good thing," he says and tugs me to him. I collide against his big warm body, and for a brief minute, a miniscule second actually, my mind goes off in a strange direction, one where Callan and I really are a couple, and happily ever after does exist.

"Callan?"

The voice comes from behind me, and Callen stiffens and lets go of my hand. I lift my gaze and turn to the guy staring at Callan like he has two heads. "What's up, Jack?" Callan says.

Jack gestures with a nod, and we follow it to see a woman and a small girl window shopping. "My wife's family has a place here. We're here for the weekend."

Callan nods and Jack turns my way. "Jack, this is Gemma,

an old friend from high school," he says, and my stomach squeezes tight, even though I have no reason to be upset. Really, we had sex, but all I am to him is an old friend from high school.

"Nice to meet you, Jack. How do you two know each other?"

"We work together," they both say in unison and I laugh.

"It's nice to see you...out," he says in a gentle way, a caring way, and I like that Callan has so many great people in his life.

"It's not—"

"Oh, I have to go, the wife is waving me over." He waves to his family. "You guys have a great weekend."

He leaves and Callan mumbles curses under his breath.

"Everything okay?"

"I just don't want him to get the wrong idea, you know. We're colleagues, and the guys at the station, well, they're all after me to get out, date more."

"I understand," I say, and continue to the store. "Maybe it's not a bad idea to let them think you are. They clearly worry about you. Maybe with us pretending, it could help you as much as it's helping me."

He nods. "You know what. You're right. You're kind of smart, Gemma."

"One of us has to be."

"Hey, I take offense to that."

I slide my arm around his back and put my palm on his chest. "Kidding, you're one of the smartest guys I know. Bravest too." As soon as those words leave my mouth, his demeanor changes, a darkness about him as a frown hijacks his face. Oh, God, what have I done? "Hey, look at this," I say, and pick up a pretty seashell necklace. "I bet Kaitlyn would love this."

He's quiet for a second, and a small smile reaches the corners of his mouth. "You think?"

"Totally, and just so you know, the piano lessons are free."

"No, they're not."

"After what you're doing for me."

He slides his arms around me, and it settles on the small of my back. His mouth is near my ear when he says, "I like doing for you."

I grin. "Doesn't matter."

"It matters, and—" I open my mouth to argue, even though I don't think it will do any good and he presses his finger to my lips. "If you want to give her free lessons, we'll figure something out. This isn't it."

"Okay, fine," I say and wonder what he has in mind. "Oh, and look at these earrings."

He frowns. "She's always wanted to get her ears pierced, but I can't seem to take her. I think if she felt any sort of pain, I'd lose my mind."

"It's not so bad and if you want, I'll take her." I search his face as he goes quiet for a moment.

"You don't have to do that."

I squeeze his arm. "And you didn't have to come here with me this weekend ."

"I'm glad I did, though." He snorts. "Maybe I am a little bit into pissing contests. I liked letting Brad know you were taken, and the only one you had to answer to was yourself."

"Did you see his face when Amanda said something about your big hose."

"Priceless," he says with a laugh. "I'm not an asshole, Gemma."

"I know that."

"Brad, though. He's an asshole. He basically told me you two were going to spend the weekend working things out."

"It's a lie."

"I know, but it speaks of his character, and that he's pretty possessive of you." His frown sends worry zinging through me.

I glance down. "I don't think he'd hurt me, though. Not physically."

"Okay, and I have to say, I probably shouldn't have taken pleasure in Amanda one upping him." He casts me a fast glance. "I'm going to Hell, aren't I?"

"Yeah, but don't worry," I say. "I'll be riding shotgun."

He laughs out loud, and it wraps around me in a comforting way. "I love that you're a ride or die kind of girl-friend," he says.

My heart jumps. *Girlfriend.* I like the sound of that...a little too much. I quickly remind myself we're each doing a favor for the other. But Callan, I don't know, it's easy to forget it's pretend at times like this.

"Okay, let's get these for Kaitlyn," he says, "And then I need to get a bathing suit and I am not stuffing myself into a ridiculous pair of speedos. I want board shorts."

"Well, of course. You need the extra room for that big hose."

He shakes his head and gives my ass a slap to get me moving. The sun is low on the horizon after we pay and step back outside. We walk a little farther until we come to a pretzel shop.

"Let's get one," he says.

I rub my stomach. "I'm still full from the barbecue earlier."

We head inside and he looks at the menus. "Will Brad be gone when we get back?"

"He'll likely be at his parents' place. I hope you're into board games. I'm sure we'll get roped into that."

He orders two pretzels, and hands me one when we step outside. I take a bite and moan. "This is good."

"See, I knew you'd want one." We make our way into the

bathing suit shop and after we get him a pair of board shorts, we head back to his car. A yawn pulls at me, and I rest my head against the seat.

"I'm looking forward to getting to bed early," I say.

"Why, you think you're going to get some sleep?" he asks, a devilish grin on his face. My heart leaps a bit. I haven't said anything, but there's no denying I've been wondering what tonight might bring. I sort of had myself convinced last night was a one-time thing.

"What are you saying, Callan?"

"If I'm here pretending to be your guy, the least you could do is have sex with me."

"The least," I say with a laugh. "I wasn't sure, Callan." I glance at him, wanting to be open and honest here.

"There's one thing I'm sure of, and I can't quite forget it."

"What's that?" I ask.

"This morning. I remember what you said you'd be willing to do in exchange for a cup of coffee."

"What did I say?"

"Oh, just something about my cock in your mouth."

"I don't believe I'd ever say something like that," I tease and wet my mouth.

"You did, and stop licking your lips like that. You're making me hard. I can't walk into your parents' place with a boner."

I put my hand over his hard cock and a tortured groan curls around me. "The ridiculous things I say before my morning cup. I'd pretty much agree to anything."

"Are you saying it's not something you want to do?"

His cock jumps beneath my hand as I lightly stroke it. "No."

He grins. "Is it something you want to do?"

I lean into him. What I'm about to do is reckless, and

inappropriate, but I like who I am with Callan. I pop his button and lower his zipper.

"What the fuck, Gemma."

I blink innocent eyes at him. "We can't have you walking around with this monstrosity in front of my family." Before he can get a word out, I bend, and he sinks to the back of my throat. I grin as he pounds on the steering wheel and curses under his breath. "That is so fucking good."

I smile as I give him pleasure, liking the way I make him feel, how encouraging his words are. I go deep, and slide my hand around his base, massaging gently. One of his hands lands on my head, his fingers raking through my hair as his hips lift an inch.

"I need to stop the car," he says, and I moan in agreement. I work my mouth over him, my lips tight around his crown before I take him to my throat again.

"Fuck, Gemma," he growls out. "You are so good at that." His words bolster my confidence, and while this is not the time to think of my ex, I can't help but think about his behavior, the way he kept me down, even belittling me in the bedroom.

His veins bulge, thicken in my mouth, and he groans louder. "You've got me right there," he growls. He tries to pull my head away, but I don't let him. I bob up and down, slide my hand into his pants to cup his balls. They tighten in my hand as I rub them gently, and his fingers grip my hair tighter as he lets go in my mouth. I drink him in, swallow every last drop. Using my tongue, I twirl it around his crown, and when he finally stops spasming, I slowly lift my head.

Callan has one hand on the steering wheel, gripping so hard his knuckles are white, and his eyes are closed, like he's in total agony. My heart leaps, and I start to second-guess my actions.

"Callan?"

He exhales and slowly opens his eyes. My worry dissipates when he casts me a glance and slowly shakes his head. "Yeah?"

I laugh. "Are you okay?"

"Of course I'm not okay," he says with a laugh. "You just gave me the best blowjob of my life, in a car, on Main Street."

"So, you liked it?"

He chuckles, puts his hand around my head, and draws my mouth to his. "I loved it," he whispers into my mouth before giving me a deep, passionate kiss.

"Good, because I loved doing it."

"Tonight, I'm going to show you what I love doing," he says, a promise in his voice.

"Ooh, can't wait."

"Although it might be weird having sex in your parents' house with them in the other room. It's like I'm a teenager again. Sneaking around for sex."

"I've actually never done that."

His brow quirks. "Really, well then we need to change that."

"I think it will be fun."

"I know it will be."

With darkness surrounding us, he starts the car, and is about to pull into traffic when a police car passes us. I don't miss the way the driver is glaring at Callan. I just know something bad is going to happen, and I don't have to be a rocket scientist to know who's behind it.

"Who the hell was that?" I ask and brace myself.

"He's coming back," I say, as the car spins around and the lights go on. "This is not good, Callan"

"It's okay. We've not done anything wrong."

"That still doesn't mean you're not going to be harassed. I'm sure Brad told his colleagues to keep an eye out for you."

"I have no doubt."

"This is why I just left, Callan. I didn't want to face these kinds of things." I grip my hands and wring them. "I'm so sorry. I never should have involved you."

"Hey," he says and covers my hands. "It's going to be fine. I can handle a little harassment and at least he's picking on someone his own size."

Callan rolls his window down as the officer approaches. "How can I help you, officer?"

"Your taillight is out."

Callan shakes his head. "I had no idea. It was fine earlier."

"Can I see your license and registration?" The officer looks into the car. "Is that you, Gemma?"

"Hi Greg," I say.

"Didn't realize you were home," he says. "Oh, wait, maybe Brad did say something about you guys hanging out this weekend." I open my mouth, about to correct him, but Callan's hand on my leg stops me.

"Here you go," he says, and hands the paperwork over.

The officer looks it over. "I'll be right back."

He disappears to his car, and Callan casts me a glance. "Yeah, Brad's behind this."

"I'm sorry."

"It's okay, I got this. You have nothing to worry about," he says, but the tightness in his jaw, the hard set of his chin, tells another story. Callan thinks I *do* have something to worry about.

9

CALLAN

I keep a smile on my face when we step back inside the beachside home, and laughter reaches our ears. Gemma smiles up at me, but there is a new kind of tension in her body. She didn't like being pulled over any more than I did. It was Brad flexing his muscle, that much I'm sure of. But what worries me the most is what else he'd do to prove he's powerful and try to win Gemma back. No way in a million fucking years is she going back with him. Even if he did win her over, but she's too smart for that, it'd have to be over my dead body.

"Looks like the board games have begun," she says. We head back outside and the deck is lit with Chinese lanterns, creating a cozy atmosphere. The kids are all in bed at this hour, and the adults are sitting around the table with their favorite drinks.

"How was the shopping?" Amanda asks when she sees the bags in our hands.

"Good," I say. "I got some swim trunks and a T-shirt for both me and my daughter. I also got her a seashell necklace that Gemma thought she'd love."

Amanda's jaw drops. "You have a daughter?"

I stiffen for a second. Is Gemma dating a man with a child going to be a problem for them? Not that we're really dating, I remind myself. I almost forget there for a second that it wasn't real.

"He does," Gemma says. "Kaitlyn, she's six, and goes to my school." She smiles up at me. "And I'm going to be teaching her piano."

Amanda glares at me and plants one hand on her hip. "Why didn't you bring her? I would love to meet her and she could have played with the kids."

"You're right. I should have. But this is the week she spends with her grandparents. They've been looking forward to it."

Amanda relaxes. "Okay, you're off the hook." She points a finger. "Next time, though."

I laugh and hold my hands up in surrender. "Yup, next time," I say, although I doubt there will be one. I just hope Brad eventually gets the message and backs off.

"Can I see what you got her?" Janice asks.

"Oh Mom, its adorable. She's going to love it." Gemma takes the bag from me and opens it. As the women all admire the delicate piece of jewelry, David catches my eye.

"Scotch?" he asks holding his glass up.

"Love one," I say.

"Come give me a hand," he says, and we head inside to the bar. I drop the rest of my bags on the kitchen counter.

"Ice?" David asks, and when I hear the remnants of his tinkling in his glass, I say, "Sure," and wonder what this is all about. Am I going to get the big brother 'talk'? If so, I'm wondering if he ever gave it to Brad.

"Amanda told me she remembers you from when you and Gemma went to high school together." I nod as he hands me my glass.

"Yeah, we're old friends."

"I'm glad you're here, Callan."

I angle my head and take a sip from my glass. "Why is that?"

"I never liked that asshole Brad. I could never put my finger on it, but he always rubbed me the wrong way."

Gemma never told anyone about his behavior, but clearly a few members of the household are intuitive. "You don't have to worry about him, David," I say.

He nods, and holds his glass up to mine. "Glad to hear it."

We clink glasses and are about to head back outside when Gemma steps inside. Her gaze goes back and forth between the two of us. "David, you better not be giving him a hard time," she says but there is a teasing, loving warmth between the two. He rubs his knuckles on her head and she swats his hand away.

"Just getting to know your new guy, that's all."

"Did Amanda put you up to this?"

He shakes his head like she might be crazy. "Of course she did," he says and the two burst out laughing. He shrugs. "Big sisters."

Gemma huffs out an exasperated breath. "You don't always have to do what she says, you know."

He blinks once, twice, his mouth agape. "Ah, did you just meet her? Are you new here?"

"Okay, okay," Gemma says and as they laugh again, my heart pinches. My daughter has a lot of people in her life, but there is no doubt she'd love it here. Gemma grabs a bottle of wine and a glass. "Let's go have some fun playing Cards Against Humanity."

We head back outside, and I sit down next to Adam, who is Nicole's husband. He's the strong, silent type, but I like him. In fact, I like all these people.

"Is everything ready for the race tomorrow?" Nicole asks.

She glances at the sky. "I think we're going to get some sprinkles."

"Rain or shine, you know how it goes," Janice says. "I finished making the cards this evening after dinner."

"What kind of race?" I ask as Gemma shuffles the cards.

"Ooh, we have a rookie," Amanda says loudly. She rubs her hands together and glances at David. "No way can a rookie beat five-time champions."

"Sounds like a challenge," I say. "I'm always up for a challenge."

Amanda grins at me. "It's on Callan."

Gemma nudges me. "Mom and Dad put together a list of challenges, like the show Amazing Race, and we all compete. It's super fun, but I think Amanda and David cheat." She snarls at her sister and brother in law. "They win every year."

"We do not cheat," Amanda says, all indignant, and everyone laughs and rolls their eyes.

"You might think Callan here is a rookie, but you're forgetting what he does for a living," Gemma says, coming to my defense. "The man runs into burning buildings. I'm sure he can find a seashell on the sand."

"Okay, want to make a side bet?" Amanda says.

I lean toward her. "Go ahead."

She taps her chin. "If we win, you take us to dinner back in the city. If you win, we take you."

Gemma gives me a nervous glance. When this weekend is over, so is the pretend relationship, but I like her family, and a double date would be fun. Also, I need to keep her close, just to make sure her ex keeps his distance. I'm not sure how I'll go about that, but I'll have to figure out a way for her to agree.

"It's on," I say. "I can't remember the last time someone took me out for surf and turf," I tease, and Gemma laughs. She deals the cards and for the next hour over drinks and laughs, we play. We all have tears in our eyes by the time we finish.

"That game never gets old," Jim says and stretches his arms out. "I think it's my bedtime."

"Same for us," Amanda says. "We need our rest, so we can celebrate hard after we win tomorrow."

David just smirks at me, and everyone gives hugs to each other before heading inside. Gemma gathers up the cards and games and I sit back to take a breath. I love everything about this. Hard.

"You good?" Gemma asks when we're alone.

"I am. I was just thinking, maybe we could take that swim."

"I'd like that," she says. I help her carry the games inside, and snatch my bags from the counter. We pad quietly up the stairs and into her bedroom. She opens her bag and tugs out her bathing suit and I simply sit on the bed and watch her, the vision before me a thing of beauty.

"I'll be right back," she says, and I capture her arm, not wanting her out of my sight for even a second.

"Where are you going?"

She points to the ensuite bathroom. "To get changed."

I chuckle. "Babe, I've been inside you. You don't need to run away to get changed."

Pink invades her cheek. "I know." Her hands fall. "I don't know what I was thinking."

"I do."

I pull her to me, and she stands in between my spread legs. My mouth is right there, inches from her sweet nipples.

"You do?"

"Yeah, I do."

"What was I thinking, then?" she asks, not even bothering to hide the arousal in her voice or her body.

"You were thinking you gave me the best head in the car

today, and that maybe it was my turn to put my tongue and mouth all over your beautiful body." She quakes and I hold her tight to absorb the tremors. I tear my gaze away from her hard nipples poking through her T-shirt and her eyes are dark, half mast, when she dips her head to see me. Her hair tumbles over her shoulders, and I push it back to expose the long column of her neck.

Her long lashes fall slowly and rise again. "Yeah, I might have been thinking that."

"Might have? No vagueness with me, Gemma. You need to straight up tell me the truth."

"You want the truth, Callan?"

I hear a sexy little hitch in her voice, and her chest rises and falls as she grows breathless.

"Yes."

She rakes her hands through my hair. "Okay. Last night. Sex with you. I've never experienced that kind of pleasure before. My body hasn't stopped humming all day. I'm trying hard to focus on other things, trying hard to make conversation with family, but it's near impossible, I crave to be touched by you again. I want your mouth on me, your fingers and cock inside me. I want it all, with you. Sex with Brad was rough, almost violent. I was terrified, to tell you the truth. I never wanted to have sex, but somehow always found myself beneath him. He never worried about my pleasures, or my body. I never knew sex could be...nice."

"I won't hurt you, Gemma."

"I know. The way you made me feel last night, important and beautiful. It was so nice." Her hand cups my face. "I appreciate all you're doing for me."

"You *are* all those things, Gemma. No one should ever have taken them away from you. Plus, I'm kinda sorta doing it for me too," I admit. "It's not like I'm not getting something out of this," I say, and she chuckles.

My heart pounds, loving the way she's open with me, but my insides are in turmoil, wanting to hunt down her ex and beat the motherfucker. She's clearly kept so many secrets, hid so much pain. I want to be the guy to bring out her confidence, watch her blossom under my touch, and show her that sex between two people who care about one another should be a beautiful thing, not something to fear.

"There's one more thing I'm wondering about," she says, and purses her lips.

I grip her waist, and span my fingers. "What's that?"

"I'm wondering if maybe you want to skip the swim."

"Swimming is so overrated," I tell her and her warm chuckles tug on my balls. I stand, and my body brushes hers the whole way up. I grip her T-shirt and peel it over her head. Today she's wearing a lacy black bra, and I can't help but think this is for me.

I bend and bury my face between her breasts, breathing in the scent of her skin. I rub my thumbs over her lace. "Mmm, I like," I say and slide my hand around her back. "But this, I like even more," I add when her bra slides from her body. I stand back, take in her gorgeous breasts. I must take too long staring. She shifts and her hands go to cover herself up.

"No, Gemma. Don't hide from me." She nods and slowly lowers her hands. "You're so goddamn beautiful. Do you have any idea what you do to me?" I ask.

She glances at my cock pressing hard against my pants. "I'm pretty sure I do."

"And you like that, right?" I don't have to ask, but I do, just to hear her say it.

She grins. "I do."

I smile at that. I had no idea how badly I needed a woman's touch until our lives collided, literally. I can't help but wonder if any woman's touch would fill my soul the way hers does. That frightens me a little, to be honest. I don't deserve happiness, or want to take any kind of pleasure from life. Not when I couldn't save my own wife and unborn son. I swallow as pain flashes through me, my entire body tightening.

"Callan," Gemma says in a soft voice. I lift my head, and our eyes latch. As if she knows every dark thought inside me, she presses a light kiss to my mouth. "Let's get out of our heads, okay? Just me and you. No one else but the two of us, right here, right now. What we're doing is right. It's right, Callan."

"I know," I say, not questioning it either. I feel this every bit as much as she does. "I need you, Gemma," I say. I rip my shirt off and pull her to me. I slide my hands up her back, and grip her shoulders, needing the skin-on-skin contact. "I need you so bad."

"You've got me," she whispers into my ear. "Just like I've got you."

I inch back and kiss her, deeply, passionately, opening up a part of me that had been closed off for two full years. It's frightening, but it's also so fucking nice. The tension in my shoulders lessen, and I revel in the sensations racing through me as she runs her hands down my back, offering herself to me. The fact that this woman is opening up to me after her past experiences isn't something I take lightly, and I plan to do right by her.

My mouth leaves hers, tracks down her body until I'm sitting on the bed, and she's quivering on her legs before me. I rip open the button on her shorts, and peel them down her legs.

"Gemma."

"Yes," she says as I tug my phone from my pocket.

"Are you calling someone," she asks, and starts to wrap her hands around her body.

"No." I set my phone on the bed. "Do you feel beautiful?"

"I..." She glances into my eyes. "Yes."

I smile and nod at that. "When was the last time you danced?"

She shakes her head and looks down. "It's been a long time, Callan."

That breaks my fucking heart. "Did dancing make you feel good...free?"

"Yeah, I miss it, actually."

"Would you dance for me?" I ask, and her head jerks back.

Her breath comes a little fast. "You were serious about that?"

"Yes."

"I don't know, Callan." She looks down at her feet. "I'll feel silly."

"I'll start with you." I flip through my apps and put on a song, an old one from our high school days and she laughs.

"Why is that on your phone?" she asks, her body relaxing.

"The women at the station got hold of my phone one day," I say.

"Liar. You just like the oldies."

"I admit to nothing." I set my phone down and take her into my arms. "But you should see the pic they added to my wallpaper." I roll my eyes and laugh. "They had fun that day, and taught me a valuable lesson. Keep my phone locked."

She chuckles and puts her head on my chest as we move to the slow song. "I think I like these women already."

"They're going to love you," I say, and my throat tightens as I hold her against me. They *are* going to love her. Heck what's not to love.

Whoa, easy, Callan. This is all just pretend.

My cock thickens as I hold her to me, her body swaying and stroking me in places so deep, it's almost frightening. I honestly can't remember the last time I was this happy. Gemma helps me forget about the real world for a while, but it's there for me to go back to once this weekend is over. I must say, though, after a taste of this, it's going to be fucking hard going to bed alone, waking up alone. Again.

As she relaxes in my arms, I step back and sink back onto the mattress. She bites her bottom lip, and stills.

"Dance for me, Gemma," I murmur.

Dressed in nothing but black lace panties, she begins to sway her hips, her beautiful breasts jutting out, her nipples so pink and puckered, my mouth waters. Jesus, I like her. She is the most beautiful woman on the planet. But she's more than just beauty. So much more.

She grips the thin elastic band with her thumbs and tugs. All thoughts dissipate as my blood rushes south. "Hmm," I say.

"You like that, Callan?"

"Uh huh," is all I can manage to push past my lips.

She turns around, and presents me with her lush ass. As she shakes it, I remove the rest of my clothes, until I'm stark naked. I take my cock into my hand, and her eyes go wide when she turns back to face me.

"You like this?" I ask as I tug from base to tip.

"I do," she says, her gaze latched on my cock.

I want my hand in those panties, but I need to see her naked. "Get rid of the panties. I want to see your pussy," I say.

She bends forward, and a growl rips from my throat as she sheds the last of her clothes. Moving slowly, she stands back up again and continues to sway.

"Open yourself up. I want to see all of you."

She reaches between her legs, and using her fingers, she spreads her damp lips. I almost weep. "Fuck, Gemma," I gulp.

"You like?"

"Yeah, I like."

She rubs her clit, and moans as she slides a finger into herself.

"I have a confession," she whispers.

"Tell me."

"Many years ago, I used to touch myself, imagining it was you."

Jesus Christ, I can't believe she's admitting that to me. "You did?" I ask, excited by that.

"Yeah."

"Well, you don't have to imagine it anymore." I stand, slide one arm around her as the other goes between her legs. I move her finger, and replace it with mine. I slide deep inside her, stretching her soaked walls, and lightly rubbing the bundle of nerves that sets her on a path to ecstasy. She's so damn hot and wet, she nearly orgasms right there. I fucking love it.

"That's so good," she says and sags against me. I hold her upright and fuck her with my fingers slowly.

"Are you going to come all over my fingers?" I ask.

"You keep that up and I am."

I press the butt of my hand against her clit and massage it. She grips my shoulders and a cry catches in her throat. "I want that too, but I also want you to ride me and come all over my cock. I want to hold your hips and pull you down, feel you squeeze around me. Mostly, I want to see your face when your sweet pussy takes every inch of me inside you."

My words do something to her. Her nails dig into me, and her body spasms around my finger. "Fuck, I love watching you come," I say as she pulses and clenches and comes some more. The second her tremors subside, I lower myself onto the bed and position her on top of me, until her legs are on either side of my body. I lift her and drag her up until her pussy is over my mouth.

"Sit on my face," I tell her and she takes her breasts into

her hands and lowers herself until her juices soak my mouth. I lap and eat at her, and suck her sensitized clit until she's moaning in pleasure again. She rides my face shamelessly and I fucking love it. Her hips move, back and forth, as she grinds on my tongue.

As my cock aches, I slowly lift her and reposition her. Seconds before I'm about to pull her down, plunge high inside, some brain cell reminds me I need a condom. "Fuck, Gemma. Condom. My bag."

Face flushed, she pushes her mess of hair from her shoulder. "Actually," she says, breathless. "I have some in my bag."

I grin at that. "You thought ahead."

"When you insisted on *coming* with me," she teases, "I found some I had and they're not expired."

"Brains and beauty, how the fuck did I get so lucky?"

She laughs at that, and climbs from my body, and I instantly miss her warmth. "Hurry back," I say and take my cock into my hand. She bends over to root in her bag, pointing her sweet ass at me and I growl.

"Jesus, Gemma. You got a thing about shaking that ass at me?"

"You don't like?" she asks innocently as she stands with a condom in her hand.

"You tell me," I say and gesture to my cock.

She slowly crawls back on to the bed, and goes between my legs. "Poor guy needs some attention." She takes me to the back of her throat, and I grab a fistful of her hair as she sucks on me. I pull her off and her grin is coy. Yeah, she knows exactly what she's doing to me.

"You're a tease, Gemma."

"Who, me?"

I laugh. I loved my wife, I loved having sex with her, but I don't ever remember laughing. I like this. A lot.

"Put that condom on me already," I growl.

"Such an impatient man," she says.

"Have you seen yourself?" I say. "Can you blame me for wanting my cock inside you sooner rather than later?"

She rolls the condom down the length of me, and I reach for her, pull on her until she's straddling me. "Open your pussy," I say, and she parts herself with her fingers, a sweet invitation if I ever saw one. "Tell me what you want," I say as she tries to lower herself, but I keep hold of her hips to prevent her from burying my cock inside her.

She moans her disapproval as I continue to prevent her from moving. "I want you, Callan. I want this gorgeous cock inside me."

I let her hips go and she sinks down, taking every last inch into her hot, tight body. "Fuck." I groan.

"Exactly."

She twirls her hips, and my balls ache for release as she clenches around me. I take her breasts into my hands and knead gently. She arches into my touch, her eyes half-mast. I sit up, licking her nipple, sucking on it gently and twirling it between my teeth. Her hands go around my head and she holds me to her as her hips continue to move, rotate. I put one hand behind me and power up.

"Oh," she says breathlessly as I piston in and out of her, changing the pace and rhythm, wanting her cum all over my cock.

I fall back to the bed, and grip her hips again, taking pressure off her thighs as she rides me. With each downward thrust, she grinds her clit on my pelvis, and it's all I can fucking do to hang on, but before I let go, I want her juices all over me.

Her head goes back, her hair wild around her shoulders, and it rattles my control. I muster every ounce of strength I can possess to hang on, but every movement, the sexy way she writhes against me, torments every bone in my body. My muscles tense, everything in the way she's taking my cock totally fucking wrecking me. I hit her deep, and she moans.

"Callan," she cries out, and when she realizes how loud that was, she glances at me and bites her lips.

I grin at her as we bang like two hormonal teenagers and pray to fucking God her family can't hear us. "Take what you need," I say, my voice much lower than hers. "Ride my cock, Gemma. Take it deep."

She lifts, drops down onto me, and I gasp, meeting each thrust until I'm practically buried in her balls-fucking-deep. I briefly close my eyes, but open them again, absolutely blown away by how amazing she feels. I'm so fucking close, I sit up, and pull her mouth to mine. I slide my tongue into her mouth and her body lets go around me. Her body spasms around me and her hot cum sizzles over my cock and drips down my thighs.

"Gemma," I say into her mouth as sparks dance before my eyes, my own powerful explosion rocketing through me, leaving me perfectly satisfied, perfectly content.

Perfectly into this woman.

GEMMA

The sound of children playing pulls me awake, and I reach across the bed, happy to find Callan beside me. I roll to face him as his chest rises and falls with his easy breathing. My heart squeezes in my too-tight chest and I swallow against a dry throat. He is such a good guy, the best guy I know, and it hurts to think he plans to spend the rest of his life alone.

He opens one eye, and then the other, and a smile splits his lips when he finds me up on my elbow staring at him. "Hey," he says his voice sleepy and groggy. "How long have you been awake?"

"Not long," I say, and lightly trace his nipple. "I hope I didn't wake you."

"Of course you woke me. I could feel you lying there staring at me like some sort of creeper." I laugh at that and he quivers and grabs my hand to stop my exploration of his nipple. "That tickles," he says.

I laugh. "Now you know how I feel."

"Oh, are you saying you don't like it when I do this?" He reaches out to circle my nipple.

"Not exactly." I exhale a satisfied sigh, my body warm and so satiated, I'm not sure I ever want to leave the comfort of my bed.

"How are you feeling?" he asks.

I stretch out. "Glorious, you?"

For a brief second, something that looks like pain and guilt flashes in his blue eyes before he blinks it away. "I'm good," he says, but his voice lacks conviction. I let my mind drift to last night, and all the other times his deep sadness penetrated my skin and wrapped around my heart. He misses his wife, and that's totally understandable, but every intuition in me tells me there is more going on with him. I give that more thought, and that's when it hits me. He feels responsible somehow for his wife's death.

"Callan?"

"Yeah?"

"Can I ask you something?" I fluff my pillow and lay on it sideways. He does the same.

"Sure."

"How come you don't want to ever have a relationship again? Don't you think Zoe would want you to be happy?"

He rolls to his back, rests his arm on his forehead and stares at the ceiling. My entire body tightens. I don't want to hurt him anymore than he's already hurting, or for him to think he's doing his daughter an injustice by avoiding relationships, but I hate to see him spend his life alone—thinking he's somehow to blame.

"There are things you just don't know, Gemma."

"I understand that. As your friend, I'm here to talk to if you want. If you don't want to talk, that's okay too. I just want you to know I'm here for you. No judgement."

He goes quiet for a long time, and the sound of the kids playing in the yard fills the silence inside the room. I lay there, not wanting to move or breathe, and when he finally breaks the quiet, my heart jumps into my throat.

"I couldn't save her."

I take a few shallow breaths and wait for him to continue. When he doesn't, I say, "She was in a car accident, Callan. There was nothing you could do."

"No, you're wrong. I'm a first responder. I save people all the time. It's what I do." He opens his mouth, but a garbled sound catches in his throat. "It's what I do, Gemma."

The pain of his loss, the weight he carries on his shoulders, mushrooms inside me. Sorrow fills all my dark corners, and I touch him lightly. He flinches slightly, so I take my hand back. "I'm so sorry it happened."

He nods as hurt, sorrow, sadness and loss move over his face. He takes my hand and pulls it back, like he needs the connection. "I know." His head slowly turns my way. "She was pregnant."

I suck in a fast breath, my stomach coiling so tight, I think I might throw up. I shift a bit closer to offer my warmth, sensing he's opening up to me and telling me something he's never told another. There is so much going on inside this man, things he keeps from the world, things he buries and hides by using humor. He'd come here with me, running to my rescue, but from the vulnerability and pain in his eyes, it's easy to tell he's the one in need of rescuing. "Callan, I didn't know."

"No one did. We were waiting to announce it." He makes a noise, a humorless laugh, as a pained smile twists his lips. "Zoe had this whole thing planned. We had T-shirts with pizzas on them, two slices missing. Kaitlyn had a T-shirt with one slice. People were supposed to figure out why there were two slices missing."

"I get it," I say. "It's clever."

"Yeah..."

His voice trails off, and I lay my head on his chest, leaving him to his thoughts. His strong heart beats rapidly beneath my cheek and he puts his arms around me, absorbing my warmth and comfort. We stay like that for a long time, and soon enough we hear cars pulling into the driveway as friends and family gather for the day's adventures. I don't move and neither does he. If he needs me to stay here with him for the rest of the day, the weekend, then so be it. There is nowhere else I'd rather be.

Deep sadness moves over his face. "I like being with you, Gemma."

"But you don't think you deserve it," I say, voicing his thoughts when he can't. He doesn't answer, so I simply wrap my arms around him and hold him tighter. Callan is one of the nicest yet toughest guys I know, but deep inside he's raw, stripped bare. He's shouldering a lot of responsibility and guilt. It's no wonder he can't move forward when he can't come to terms with the past.

"I can't give you more than this," he says.

"I know, I'm not asking. I have a lot of healing to do myself. But Callan, eventually I hope you can move on. I'd love to see you have a family again. If anyone is a family man, it's you."

"I loved having a family. I just can't do that anymore. A wife, and more kids...what if I couldn't...I'm just. It doesn't feel right." He goes quiet again for a long time. "I promised to keep them safe," he mumbles.

"It wasn't your fault, Callan," I say gently. "You deserve happiness. Zoe would want that. I know she would."

"She was on her way to the doctor for a checkup. I was supposed to go, but got tied up with some paperwork. She told me it was okay, she was easy and independent like that... but if I would have been with her, then maybe..."

"Then maybe Kaitlyn wouldn't have a mother or a

father." I go quiet for a moment to see if he's going to allow me to continue, because yeah, I'm overstepping here, but this guy needs to talk, and right now I want nothing more than to be the friend he needs. When he remains silent, I restart with, "I know it doesn't feel that way, and I know my words aren't going to matter or change your mind, but you need to know the only one who blames you is you. Zoe was in a terrible accident. No one could have done anything. The police, the doctors, the firefighters...her husband."

"The counsellor said the same thing, and so do the members of my single parent support group." He turns to me. "Gemma," he says, his voice almost panicked.

"Yeah."

"All of this, everything I just told you is between us, okay?"

"Of course, Callan. You don't even have to say that."

He frowns and grips a fistful of his hair. "I'm not even sure why I opened my mouth."

"Because you needed to, and your secrets are safe with me, just like I know mine are safe with you."

He smiles, pushes my hair from my face, and drops a soft kiss onto my mouth. His mood shifts, and I can finally breathe again. "Don't we have a race to win?"

"We don't have to—"

"Are you kidding me?" He holds his hand up, one finger out. "One, I'm looking forward to a free meal in the city when we win, and two, let's go show douche-bag how good of a team we make."

I smile. "We do make a good team."

"Let's do this then." He glances at the clock on the night-stand. "When does it start?"

"Any time now, but we should shower." I jerk my thumb toward the ensuite bathroom. "Do you want to go first?"

He shakes his head, a small, sexy grin turning up the corners of his mouth. "Did you really just ask me that?"

"Yeah, sort of why?" I ask, as that playful smirk sizzles over my flesh like a hot caress. "What am I missing?"

"We can shower together."

"Oh, right," I say, not used to this kind of attention from a man, but loving every second of it. After sex, Brad showered alone, and I was grateful, needing quiet time to sort through all the horrible things I was feeling. With Callan, there are no bad feelings, only happy memories.

He shoves the blankets off, comes around to my side and takes my hand. He lifts me from the bed, and my naked body collides with his. He groans. "Maybe showering together is a bad idea."

"Oh, hang on a second," I say, and turn, his morning boner pressing into my ass as I lean forward and fuss with the sheets. "I always like to make my bed in the morning."

"The only thing you're making...is my cock hard."

I try to stifle a chuckle, loving that his mood is lighter and hoping somehow, some way, if not today, then down the road, he'll take my words to heart and learn to hold on to the past in a way that still allows him to have a future.

"Oh, I didn't know."

"Sure you didn't," he says and I yelp when he scoops me up and marches me into the bathroom. "Do you think they'll mind waiting a bit longer?" he growls into my ear as he turns the water on and adjusts the temperature.

"Do they even have a choice?"

"No," he says and squirts a generous amount of soap into his hand to wash me. I sigh as his big, warm hands race over my body, touching and cleaning every inch of me. He puts his fingers between my legs, and lightly strokes my sensitized clit. My head falls back against his chest.

"Callan, that feels incredible."

His mouth is close to my ear, his breath hot on my neck when he says, "Put your hands on the wall."

Without question, I step away from him and do what he's asked. He growls.

"Spread your legs."

I widen my legs and tip my ass up to him, and I'm rewarded with a thick finger inside me. He strokes me deep, but it's not enough. I need his cock.

"Callan, please fuck me."

He growls and I glance over my shoulder to see him take his big, fat cock into his hand. He strokes himself. "This what you want?" he asks.

"Yes," I murmur.

He steps up to me and positions himself near my opening. His strong fingers grip my hips, and he powers forward, filling me so thoroughly, so deeply, it steals the breath from my lungs.

His hands circle my body and he cups my breasts, squeezing them as he moves inside me. I push back, wanting him deeper, wanting everything. My God, I love this man's cock inside me. Love the way he takes me.

"Just like that," I say and lick my lips. My fingers claw against the tiled wall as he holds my hips tight and changes the pace and rhythm until my legs nearly give way. But he's there behind me, holding tight so I don't fall.

I gulp, as pleasure centers between my legs. Small ripples spread from my core, to my sex, and I clench hard around his pumping cock as the dam breaks and I release all over him.

"Fuck yes," he says into my ear. He pulls out, slides all the way in again, and his cock swells, as he tumbles into his own orgasm. "Yeah," he murmurs, and I look at him over my shoulder loving the look on his face when his walls crumble and he gives into the pleasure.

He lifts me to my full height, until my back is against his

chest, and with his cock still inside me, he walks me backward until we're both under the spray. My sex continues to throb, until he slides from me, and as I revel in my post-orgasmic bliss, one working brain cell kicks in.

"We didn't use a condom," I murmur.

He goes completely still. "Shit." His hands go to my shoulders and he turns me to face him, and my heart clenches at the pained look on his face. "Gemma..."

"It's okay, Callan," I say quickly. "I'm actually on the pill."

He exhales a fast breath, his relief palpable. "Thank God."

The man really does not want any more kids. Maybe it's more like he's afraid to put himself out there again, afraid of loving and losing. After having his life ripped out from beneath him, I can understand that.

"I use a condom for other reasons," I say.

"I'm clean, Gemma," he says, his eyes searching my face. "I've not been with anyone in years, as you well know."

My heart wobbles a little and I'm glad that I'm the one he chose to be with after all this time. "I'm clean too."

"I know," he says, and brushes his knuckles over my cheek, the gesture so soft and tender, my heart can't help but want to get involved. "That was..." He gives a low, slow whistle.

"Fun," I say.

"Yeah, but..." He frowns as his words fall off. "But it was also really...nice."

"It was nice," I say and go up on my toes to press a soft kiss to his mouth, tugging that luscious bottom lip between my teeth, leaving a mark on him. When I let go, he runs his tongue over his bruised lip.

"We should get a move on."

"Wait," I say. "It's Sunday. When are you back to work?"

"Not until Wednesday."

Relief races through me. It's probably not great that I'm

not ready for this weekend to be over. "Is being here keeping you from things that need your attention?"

"Well, actually yeah. It kind of is."

My heart sinks. "If you have to go—"

He presses his fingers to my lips and chuckles. "Playing games with your family is keeping me from this," he says and lightly runs his finger over my sex. "This is what needs my attention."

"Oh," I say and laugh at his playfulness. "You can give *that* all the attention it needs later tonight. Actually, maybe we can take the boat out this afternoon. That would be fun."

"Look at you, wanting to get all creative."

"I've got you for a little longer, Callan. I plan to take full advantage of you."

He laughs, shuts the water off and steps from the shower. "They're going to know, Gemma. One look at us and they're going to know what's been keeping us." He wraps a towel around me and helps me out.

I shrug. "We're adults, doing what adults do. If we have sex written all over us, then Brad really will get that it's over."

"Okay, then. Let's head on down. You go ahead first. I'm going to check in with my folks and Kaitlyn."

I dress, head into the bathroom to comb and tie my hair back, and then make my way downstairs to give him privacy to talk to his daughter. As I leave the room, I hear the pleasure in his voice as he talks to his little girl that means so much to him, and it brings a smile to my face. He's such a great dad. I touch my stomach, wonder at the joy of motherhood. It's something I want, something Brad and I talked about early on, before I saw his true, possessive nature.

I lightly brush my hand over my stomach, the thoughts of my own child making me smile, but that's when a horrible thought hits. I forgot to take my birth control yesterday. After sleeping over at Callan's the night before, and rushing to get here, it slipped my mind completely, but I'm sure we're fine. I turn back at the foot of the stairs and sneak into the room to grab my purse. Callan is sitting on the bed, frowning, staring at the phone in his hands.

I'm about to leave but turn back around. "Is everything okay," I ask, worry zinging through me.

His head lifts. "Kaitlyn is fine, and so are my parents."

"What's wrong?"

"Nothing I can't fix, really." He pushes off the bed. "My babysitter messaged. She just accepted an au pair position overseas. I'm going to have to find a new nanny for the summer. I'll put a couple calls in to the agency tomorrow morning when it opens. Not much I can do about it right now."

I nod, and bite my bottom lip. If he was stuck, I could help out. I mean, look at how he's helping me. It would be a good way to pay him back. I'm about to offer when my phone pings. I search my purse, but it's not there. Now where did I put it. I thought it was in here. Callan lifts my phone from the nightstand.

"You put it here."

"Right, I forgot." I read my sister's message.

Amanda: If you two can keep your hands off each other for five minutes, we'd like to get started.

I shove my phone into my purse and chuckle as heat warms my cheeks, no doubt turning pink.

"We'd better go," I say.

Callan gives me a slap on the ass to set me into motion. We hurry downstairs and while family and friends are outside, we find Amanda in the kitchen waiting for us.

"About time," she says, and pours us each a big mug of coffee.

"You're the best," I say, and she laughs as I sit to enjoy the first few sips.

"About time you realized that, too." Her smile drops.

"What?" I ask.

She nods toward the deck. "Brad is back."

I take another sip of my coffee. "I figured he would be. He loves to hang out here for some reason."

"The reason is because he wants you back, which makes it strange that he's here with someone."

"Someone?" I ask, my pulse jumping a notch.

She drops down beside me. "Yeah, a fellow officer, I believe. I'm not sure what that's all about. But right now, the two of them are giving the kids rides in the cop car." Just then a siren sounds from outside.

"I guess it's about making me jealous so I come to my senses and run back to him." I glance at Callan and find him watching me carefully. "I really wish he would find someone and move on." I honestly don't think he's fighting for me back because he loves me. I think it's more that he hates that I left, that he's threatened by his ultimate lack of control—being left by someone. I've read enough articles about the behavior, and some say the threats could increase after leaving. Other than constantly messaging me, though, nothing has really frightened me, and with Callan here, I feel completely safe.

I grab a muffin from the platter in the center of the table and hand it to Callan. "Let's hope he gets it today," Callan states before he bites into the fruit-filled muffin.

"You good, Gemma?" Amanda asks.

"Of course." I reach out and put my hand on Callan's. "How could I not be good when I have Callan here with me?"

"You know, I have a confession," Amanda says, a sheepish grin on her face.

We both look at her. "What?" I ask.

"When I first saw you and Callan together, I had this weird feeling he was here, I don't know, like a pretend boyfriend or something." She rolls her eyes. "I clearly watch too many rom coms. But I thought this set up was a way to get Brad off your case and let him know once and for all that you were done with him." She smiles. "But now...seeing you two together. I can see I was wrong."

"You were?"

"You two really care about each other. It's easy to tell."

I swallow. I hate lying to my sister and family, and honestly, am I really lying at all? I care about Callan and if he didn't care about me, he wouldn't be here helping.

She presses her hands on the table and stands. "Of course, I didn't need to *see* it with my own eyes to know."

"What's that supposed to mean?"

She gives me a sly grin. "Oh, just that my room is next to yours, in case you forgot, and my *ears* told me how crazy you two are about each other."

I groan at her crassness, my gaze going to Callan. We might be fibbing about our relationship, but my sister is right about one thing.

I *am* crazy about him.

GEMMA

By the time I step outside with my sister, Brad is back from giving the kids a ride. I instantly feel his eyes drilling into my back. I glance over my shoulder, but Callan's phone was ringing, so he stayed behind to answer it. Without him by my side, Brad steps away from the pretty brunette who's shooting daggers my way, and cups my elbow.

"Can we talk?" he asks, his dark eyes narrow, his body tight.

I pull away from him. "I really have nothing to say, Brad, and your girlfriend doesn't seem very happy that you're talking to me."

His teeth clench, the muscles in his jaw rippling as I provoke his temper. Not that it takes much. He was always angry about one thing or another, always putting me down for not doing this or that right.

"Yeah, well, I have something to say to you." He reaches out and touches my arm, and all my nerve endings jump, and not in a good way. "I want you back, Gemma. We were good together."

"It's over, Brad." I step back, putting a measure of physical and emotional distance between us. "I'm with Callan now."

"Since when?" he asks, a smirk playing on his lips like he has a secret.

I glance at the door again, waiting for Callan to come outside. Truthfully, it's not even because I need his help with Brad, it's because I actually miss him. Cripes, I've only been away from him for a few seconds and I miss him. "Long enough to know he's the guy for me," I say with a lift of my chin.

He scoffs. "Yeah, I don't think so."

"What's that supposed to mean? Have you been watching me?" Unease creeps down my spine, and I wrap my arms around myself. My God, I think he's been keeping tabs, and that's just messed up. My first thought is to go to the police, until I remember he's a cop, and I don't think any good could come from that.

"Let's just say, you guys are up to something and I plan to get to the bottom of it."

"Dig all you want. We're happy together. Anyone can see that."

He opens his mouth, no doubt to refute that, but from the lawn below the deck, Mom and Dad wave and call out, "Are you guys ready to play?"

Brad plasters on a big smile. "You bet we are," he says, and I just shake my head.

What did I ever see in him? Then again, he was always kind and charming, and my parents really encouraged me to give him a chance. It was behind closed doors where his true controlling nature came out.

Callan comes outside and slides his arm around me. I turn to him and smile.

"Everything okay?" I ask, as Brad walks away and makes his way to the lawn with his new girl, where family and friends are gathered, waiting on instructions for the race.

"Yeah, just about a change in meeting times for the support group." He gestures with a nod toward Brad as he heads down the stairs to join the others on the lawn. "What did he want?" he asks when we're alone.

I lean into him, comforted by his warmth and strength. "He said he wanted to talk."

"I won't leave you alone again."

"It's okay, I told him I have nothing to say."

"I'm still not leaving you alone." He slides his arm around my waist. "Let's go have some fun."

We make our way to the lawn, and all my aunts, uncles, sisters and husbands and their kids are paired up—the littlest ones are in strollers or their parents' arms, of course. My mom hands out the homemade cards with her written instructions for the games, and smiles at us all. She loves having everyone home and I'm really glad I came.

"We have a series of tests," she explains, and I glance around to see obstacle courses set up. They do it differently every year. This time it looks like we have to climb through a tube, swing across bars, and build something, although I can't figure out what it is until I glance at the card.

"A marshmallow launcher," Callan says with a laugh. "What is that?"

"I guess we'll figure out when we reach it."

"Oh, look a hacky sack juggle," Nicole says to her husband Adam. "Your soccer days are going to help with that one."

"You'll have to take that one, too. I can't juggle anything," I say to Callan. "Looks like we finish off with a scavenger hunt. Some fun search clues here."

"Your family really gets into this," he says with a frown.

"You don't want to play?"

"No, I do. I just wish Kaitlyn was here. She'd love this."

"Next year we will bring her, and until then, we could set something up like this at the Boys and Girls club," I say and he nods, like he too is aware that there won't be a next year for us.

"This would be a fun activity for the kids at the club," he says, cementing the fact that yeah, there will be no next year.

But I'm not going to think about that or worry about it. Right now, we're playing a role to get Brad off my back, and having fun with each other while we do it. Mom holds up a white flag as we all stand at the end of our tube.

"Ready, set go," she says, and I drop to my knees to go first. I hurry through the tunnel, feeling like a kid again and when I jump from the other side, I realize I'm the last one out. For a brief second I brace myself, then realize it's Callan I'm with and he's not about to get me in private and belittle me. It's just a game, for God's sake. I actually feel sorry for the girl with Brad, even if she looked at me like she wanted to hurl me from the deck. I wave for Callan to go. He makes it through much quicker than I do. I'm pretty good on the bars, so I finish them quickly, but my sister is still ahead of me. So is everyone else.

"I have no equal," Amanda yells, and I'm laughing so hard by the time Callan finishes the bars and we reach the marsh-mallow launcher, I can barely read the instructions.

"Here, let me," Callan says. "Okay we have a cup, a pair of scissors and a balloon." He scratches his head. "How do we make a marshmallow launcher with this?"

I stare at the supplies for a few seconds, my mind racing. "Oh, I've got it." I do numerous craft activities with the kids at school and the club so this one I can figure out pretty easily. I cut the cup and the balloon. Then I knot the balloon and tug the rubber around the cup until it's snug.

"Oh, that's cool," Callan says. "Smart girl."

I beam at the compliment. Silly, I know but he makes me feel so good about myself, and I'm honestly having a blast with him, and he doesn't really seem to care if we win or not. I like that. "Now I need to shoot three into this bucket, which you have to put on your head," I say.

"Let's do it the other way around. It will be harder for you because of my height." All around me cheers and laughter ring out as the couple and kids try to beat everyone else at getting their marshmallows into the bucket. I hold mine on my head and stand behind the line marked in the grass. I lean forward a bit to make it a bit easier for Callan.

"Cheater," Amanda calls out. "Gemma is leaning, Mom."

"Oh my God, do you have to tell Mom everything?" I say, with a laugh.

I stand to my full height, and Callan launches the first marshmallow, hitting me right in the eyeball.

"Ow," I say, and put my hand over my face.

He laughs. "I'm sorry."

"You don't sound like you're sorry." I shoot back and play-fully give him the stink eye with my one good eye.

He tries to hide a chuckle. "No, really I am."

"Oh, you're one of those are you."

He tries again and it bounces off my nose. Working hard to hide a laugh he says, "One of what?"

"You know those weird people who laugh when someone hurts themselves."

"I am not that person," he says, and launches another marshmallow. This time it goes into the bucket. "Got it," he says and cheers.

"Don't cheer yet. Amanda and David are on the move. He's nailing that hacky sack."

"We'll catch up there. I'm good at it too."

He launches a couple more marshmallows and he finally

gets them all in. We drop everything and I give David a little nudge as we pass, knocking the sack off his knee.

"Cheaters," he calls out.

"You have to start again," Mom says. "You have to get twenty in a row."

"You are so dead to me," Amanda calls out as Callan gets the sack into motion. I count them off, and he nearly fumbles at fifteen.

"Go, Callan!" I squeal and jump up and down, but something about me distracts him and he loses his concentration.

"Go David," Amanda says, and I pick the sack back up and hand it to Callan.

He puts his hand around my wrist and tugs me to him. Our bodies collide and his mouth goes to my ear. "You probably shouldn't jump up and down like that, Gemma."

"What, what did I do?" I ask, as his gaze drops to my cleavage.

"Oh," I say and chuckle, but I seriously love seeing him playful like this, and I also love the way he admires my body. "No jumping, got it," I say, and he tosses me a grin full of promise when I step back. My stupid heart does a little dance in my chest whenever I'm the sole focus of his attention. God, I really love being with him. I turn, and when I catch Brad's eye, I don't miss the way he is staring at us as his girlfriend tackles the hacky sack challenge. I work to ignore him, as well as the uneasy sensations sliding down my back. Callan starts count again.

"Later, losers," Amanda yells and disappears into the trees, with David in search of their next item. I run back to get a marshmallow and toss it at her. She dodges it and laughs.

"You're going to pay for that," I say.

"No, you are when you have to take us out to dinner. I'll probably be in the mood for a big-ass lobster."

"Twenty," Callan finally calls out, and we look over our list to figure out the scavenger items we need to find. We dart into the trees, and I nearly trip on a stump.

Callan grabs me before I go down and pulls me against him. A moan catches in my throat as my back presses to his chest and he slides his hands around my stomach.

"Got you," he says into my ear, and my pulse leaps. "You know," he teases, "if we hang back a bit, we can make out behind that tree over there." I glance at the big tree trunk.

"I've never made out in the woods before," I say.

"Time to fix that," he says and scoops me up. He hurries to the big tree, sets me on my feet and presses against me. His lips instantly find mine and I squirm against him when his cock presses against my stomach. How the hell can he be aroused again after this morning? I almost laugh at that. I'm one to talk. My panties are getting wetter by the second. He kisses me passionately, like nothing else in the world exists but the two of us, and I melt into him, lose myself in his mouth and his touches.

He breaks the kiss, and my half-lidded eyes open when he puts his finger to his mouth to quiet me. I mouth the word, "What?" and listen for sound. A second ago I couldn't hear anything other than the moans in my throat. Before he can answer, I hear it too. Footsteps close to us. "Squirrel," I whisper, and I don't know why, but that makes him laugh, hysterically.

He backs up and bends over, laughing so hard, I can't help but laugh along with him. As he laughs, it's like the world lightens for him. His shoulders are less tense, his body more relaxed than I'd ever seen it, even after sex. I'm so glad he came with me this weekend. It's been good for both of us.

"It wasn't that funny," I say when he finally stops.

"Yeah, it kind of was."

"Come on, let's go find all these items," I say, and he captures my hand as we traipse through woods, collecting pinecones and hidden painted rocks. We eventually make our way to the cold water and kick around the sand, looking for colored shells. The private beach is full of my family and friends, and I can't stop smiling. I was so dreading this and now I'm having such a great day. The sun shines down on me and I lift my face to it.

"It's hot out here," Callan says and scoops me up.

"Don't you dare," I say and put my arms around his neck.

My sisters both squeal and cheer him on. "Hey, you guys are supposed to be on my side," I yell, but it does me little good. Callan kicks his shoes off, steps into the water and winces.

"Freezing right," I yell as he goes out a bit further. I'm not too worried about him tossing me in, though. It's too cold for even him. He swings me, pretending he's going to dunk me, but he's too sweet to do it. He just likes teasing me and I like him doing it.

Before I even realize what I'm doing, I lean in and kiss him, my heart so darn full of happiness it's a bit overwhelming. He kisses me back, and when I inch back he says. "Okay fine, if you're going to be nice and kiss me like that, I won't toss you." He looks around. "Want to continue with the hunt? We can't win now, but I'm not a quitter."

He sets me back on the sand and picks up his shoes to carry them. We hunt on the beach for all the items and by the time we make it back to the deck, everyone is there, and the barbecue is going.

I don't have to ask who won. Amanda is prancing around like the queen bee, and I have to say, I'm glad it was her and not my ex, who looks like he's sulking in the corner, while his girlfriend desperately tries to make him happy. Good luck, girlfriend. Not going to happen. I just hope she gets out sooner rather than later, and honestly, I think he just brought her to make me jealous.

But I can't think about that. Not when Callan is sitting close, and asking me if I want to take the boat out. It's not his words that are intriguing me, it's the suggestive look in his eyes that has me all hot and bothered.

Yeah, I'm having way too much fun with this guy.

12

CALLAN

I steal a glance at a very tired Gemma sitting in the passenger seat as we head back to the city. She's leaning against the headrest, her eyes half closed, but there's a small smile on her face. My heart thumps a little faster as I take in her features, reliving the amazing weekend we had together. I like her family. I even liked Brad's parents.

The woman he brought was seriously all over him, and if it was to make Gemma jealous, he didn't succeed. Nothing about that man sits right with me, and while he continued to watch Gemma and me carefully, following along as we played the scavenger hunt games and ate around the table, he kept his comments to himself, although he did seem to want to talk to Gemma. I wasn't having any of that.

As if she feels me staring, she turns my way.

"Who's the creeper now?" she teases.

I squeeze her hand. "Go back to sleep."

"No, I'm okay." She sits up a little straighter. "Did you have a fun weekend?"

I grin, recalling the games we played and the fun we had. "Your family is great."

"They really are." She stretches out her arms. "I think they were pretty accepting of you, Callan. Even Aunt Donna was smitten with you by the end of it all, and she's a huge Brad fan."

"Do you think he got the idea that you're mine?"

Mine.

Jesus, as soon as that word leaves my mouth, my heart hitches. Gemma isn't mine. I was just doing her a favor this weekend. Why then, does the thoughts of life going back to the same routine, a life without her in it, leave a knot in my stomach?

She shifts, her brow furrowed as she glances at her hands, which are tightly folded on her lap. "I hope so. A few times after dinner, he tried to get me alone to talk."

"I know."

Her grateful smile wraps around me and squeezes tight. "Thanks for always being there by my side, Callan."

"My pleasure."

"Mine too," she teases as warmth colors her cheeks.

"I guess we owe Amanda and David a meal in the city, huh, seeing as they beat our asses."

She shakes her head, her hair falling from the clip at the top of her head. "You don't have to do that, you've done enough," she says.

I tap my thumb on the steering wheel. "Maybe I want to."

Careful, dude, this isn't a real relationship.

Wait, do I want it to be?

Fuck, I just don't know anymore. Even if it did, it doesn't mean she wants more. She told me she wasn't ready for anything, that she had to work on healing first. I almost snort. I should probably be trying to do the same thing, instead of living in the past, but moving on doesn't feel right. It feels like I'm betraying Zoe. I'd already let her down by not being there to protect her and our son, like I'd vowed to do.

"I was thinking," Gemma says, bringing my thoughts back.

"What's up?"

"You need a nanny. Maybe I could help out."

The way my heart squeezes with happiness doesn't go unnoticed, but having her around full time, a girl like her, one who is so easy to fall for, might not be good for my mental health. Not only that, how the hell can I be expected to keep my hands to myself?

"You don't have to do that," I say. "I'm sure the agency can find someone else."

"Maybe I want to."

I laugh. "Touché."

"Seriously, Callan." She turns in her seat. "I don't mind at all. On the nights you're working and getting home early, you won't have to drive Kaitlyn to the Boys and Girls club. She can come with me, since it's where I'm going anyway. We also talked about piano lessons. I'll be right there to give them to her."

"What about your other students?"

"They usually come to my place," she says, like she's given this a lot of thought, and has it all figured out. "They'll just come to yours instead, if that's not a problem for you."

"Well, no. I guess it would..."

"It's settled then," she says, sitting back in her seat with a smile on her face.

"It's not settled, Gemma," I say and her face drops.

She gives a fast shake of her head, her eyes big and full of regret. "I'm sorry, Callan. I didn't mean to throw this all at you and give you no choice. I'm overstepping. I get it, and of course you don't want me invading your place."

Is that what she thinks? That I don't want her around? Cripes, it's the opposite, really, and to be honest, I want to keep her close for a little while longer. I want to make sure

Brad gets the idea that we're together and stays far fucking away from her.

Is that the only reason, dude?

Of course, it's not the only reason, and that's a big fucking problem.

"Just drop me off at my place." She opens her purse like she's searching for something and I can't help but get the sense she's just trying to busy her hands. "Where the heck is my phone? What did—"

"Gemma," I say to stop her.

"Yeah?"

"Look at me."

She lifts her head and I cast her a fast glance. "It's not settled because we need to set some ground rules. That's all I meant. I want you to stay at my place."

Her eyes brighten. "Oh, what ground rules? You mean because we don't want Kaitlyn to think...." She nods. "Right, I'll take the sofa, and it's hands off."

"Wrong."

"Wrong?"

I arch a brow playfully. "I want hands on."

She nibbles her bottom lip. "You do?"

I give her a look that suggests she's dense. "Is this the first time you've met me? Are you new here?" I tease, using David's words, and she bursts out laughing.

"So how do we handle this?"

"I want you in my bed." I take the exit off the highway. "I'm one-hundred percent certain of that."

"I want that too, Callan," she says quietly, but confidently.

"Ground rules, we're careful in front of Kaitlyn. We don't want to give her the wrong idea, but when we're alone, clothes off, hands on."

"Hmm," she says all smug as she gets comfy in the seat.

"What?"

"What if I don't agree with that?"

My throat squeezes. Shit, now I'm the one who's asked for too much. "You want different rules?"

"What if I wanted to wear clothes? Sexy clothes."

The air I've been holding leaves my lungs. "I'm pretty sure I can get behind that." A little whimper catches in her throat and I know her thoughts have gone in the exact same direction as mine. My cock thickens as I revisit yesterday morning, when I got behind her in the shower and put my cock where it always wants to be...even right now.

"Are you going to tell the guys at the station you're in a relationship?" she asks. "Like we talked about."

"If you're okay with it."

"You did it for me, why shouldn't I do it for you?" We go quiet for a long time and then she laughs quietly, her thoughts elsewhere.

"Something funny?"

"I was just thinking about Amanda. Do you really think she heard us having sex that first night?"

"You weren't very quiet," I say and she whacks my stomach.

"Hey, I wasn't the only noisy one."

"Pretty sure you were," I tease and take her hand to bring it to my mouth for a kiss. "But I like that. I like knowing when I'm doing something that brings you pleasure."

"If you like it so much, maybe you should go a little faster so we can go to your room and I can show you again."

I laugh. "It's on, but I do need to stop at the grocery store first. I missed grocery day on Saturday."

"I don't mind coming with you," she says.

"You sure? I could drop you off."

"Positive. Besides if I'm staying with you, I want to pick up all my favorites. Wait, does this mean you're going to cook for me while I'm Kaitlyn's nanny?" she asks.

"Of course," I say, embracing this strange new lightness inside me. "I'm going to show you all my mad cooking skills."

"Sweet," she says, and it brings on a laugh.

"I'm also going to fuck the nanny," I say.

Her laugh curls around my chest, squeezes like a soft hug. "Sounds like that's some fantasy you've been harboring," she teases.

"Yeah, the second you suggested it, a million fantasies popped into my head." I grin. "Any chance you'll wear one of those little French maid outfits at night for me?"

She laughs, like I'm crazy but then says, "Of course, I will."

With a new lightness about me, I focus on the road, and twenty minutes later we're strolling through the grocery store, with Gemma putting all her favorites into the cart, most of it junk food.

"I'm trying to teach Kaitlyn about eating healthy," I tell her.

"It's summer, cut the kids some slack," she says with a smile and a dismissive wave.

"Jesus, Kaitlyn is going to love having you around."

So am I.

"I put some apples in there. Look, it's a big bag."

I shake my head. "Wait until you have your own kids," I say. "You'll see how hard it will be to get them to eat an apple when they have cupcakes in the cupboard."

She goes quiet, and averts her gaze as we round the corner. Shit, I didn't mean to suggest she'd be a bad mother. I think she'll be great with kids, she's a great teacher and volunteer at the Boys and Girls Club, and I can only hope down the road she finds a guy that wants what she does. "I was just kidding, Gemma." I nudge her playfully and she nearly knocks over a cookie display. "You'll be a great mom."

"Thanks," she says, and I put my arm around her and drag

her to me. Without even realizing we might have an audience, I press my lips to hers and she melts into me. Someone clears their throat and my heart sinks into my stomach when I see my sister-in-law staring at me, her eyes so big, I'm sure they're going to pop out of her head.

"Callan," she says, her gaze zinging back and forth between Gemma and me.

"Hey, Melissa," I respond, my mind racing. How is she going to feel about seeing me with another woman? Guilt eats at me, and I brace myself. "Do you remember Gemma?"

"Gemma Davis, yes of course. How are you, Gemma?" she asks, as she leans against her cart.

"I'm great, Melissa. How are you?"

"I'm good. If Callan called more, he'd know that."

Guilt once again invades. Zoe and I spent a lot of time with Melissa, and while I drop Kaitlyn off at her parents', and Melissa always calls to talk to her, I've not spent a whole lot of time with her.

"I'm sor—"

"Oh, stop, it's fine," she says. "I know you're a busy single dad, so I'll cut you some slack, and I've been busy myself getting my food truck business off the ground." Her smile is big and genuine, and my shoulders relax. "Things are good, though."

"You have a food truck?" Gemma says, clearly impressed.

"Yeah, come on by. We're over on High Street, and we're doing street tacos, and some really great food."

"I can't wait to try it."

Melissa smiles at Gemma. "I hear you're teaching at Kaitlyn's school."

"I am."

Melissa checks her watch. "I have to run. Tami will be wondering where I am." She glances around and leans into us

conspiratorially. "We haven't told Mom and Dad yet, but I asked Tami to marry me."

I bring her in for a hug. "I'm so happy for you. You two are great together."

Just like Gemma and I are great together.

She smiles, and her eyes hold warmth and happy memories as she briefly looks off into the distance. "Zoe always liked Tami. This would have made her happy."

"She's looking down on you right now and smiling, Melissa," I say.

"I know she is. I bet she's doing the same thing to you, Callan," she says and gives my arm a little squeeze. "Listen, why don't we all have a get-together soon." She turns to me. "We'll have dinner with Mom and Dad, and maybe I'll make the big announcement with family all around us. I'm sure they'd love to see Gemma again."

I nod, and she goes up on her toes to give me a kiss on the cheek. She touches my arm, gives it another little squeeze as if to tell me she's happy for me. When she's out of sight, I let out a breath.

"You okay?" Gemma asks her knuckles brushing mine in a supportive way.

"Yeah." I rake my hand through my hair. "I thought that was going to be awkward."

"I think she's happy to see you with someone, Callan. Even if this is a fake relationship," she says reminding me what it is and what it isn't. "I've always liked Melissa."

"She's a good kid." I grip the cart and head down the aisle. "Do you think it was weird for her and she was just hiding it?"

"No, I think she's happy for us, and happy that you're living your life again. You deserve that, Callan. If she was upset, she wouldn't have told you about her engagement. That's big news. She told you before her folks, and she wouldn't have invited us to her parents' for dinner if she didn't like seeing us kiss."

"Yeah, but this isn't real, so we can't really go," I say.

She nods and turns away to grab something from the shelf, and for a brief second I wonder if she might want this to be real, too. But then I remember we want different things, and even if we didn't, neither of us are ready for more, right?

We make our way down the rest of the aisle, and once we get our groceries, we head back to my place, and it's so odd how being with her in my house, meandering around the kitchen as we put things away, feels so right.

As soon as we're done, I pull her to me, and kiss her with all the need inside me.

"Wow, what was that for?" she asks as her cheeks turn a pretty shade of pink.

"I think I remember you saying something about hurrying home so you could show me what brings you pleasure."

"I don't remember saying that," she teases. "Look at you putting words in my mouth."

"That's not the only thing I'm going to be putting in your mouth," I tell her with a grin and give her a slap on the ass to set her into motion. She yelps and darts up the stairs. I follow after her, happiness welling up inside me. I haven't been this happy in a long time. Was Gemma right when we talked early the other morning? Do I deserve happiness? Is this what Zoe would want?

The truth is, the only one who seems to have a problem with me moving on...is me.

13

GEMMA

The last month has been the most glorious month of my life. I've been staying at Callan's place and sleeping in his bed. Once Kaitlyn is fast asleep, he sneaks in and warms me with his big body as he climbs between the sheets. Some nights we have the most glorious, fulfilling sex—honestly, before him I never knew sex could be so good—other nights we'd just cuddle and talk about everything and nothing. Each morning, Callan slips from the room and hits the sofa before his daughter wakes and begins her day.

Taking care of Kaitlyn has been fun, and I have to say, the more time I spend with her, the more time I think about having my own family. Only problem is, I might want the family I'm playing house with. *Might*. Okay, more like I want to make this situation between Callan and me permanent.

"Kaitlyn, grab this," I say, getting her to help me put the last of the decorations on the float we all decorated for the summer parade. She takes the banner and holds it in place as I staple it. We stand back and admire our work.

"Well done," I say, and Kaitlyn gives me a high five and

bounces off. The kids, as well as the volunteer adults, have all been working hard to put the float together, and in less than an hour, we'll all ride it as it's pulled by the fire department.

I glance up and shade the late day sun from my eyes as Callan and his crew bring the big firetruck into the empty parking lot where we're all getting organized. The world spins a little as he climbs from the truck and comes toward us. I grab onto the side of the float to keep myself upright.

"Gemma, are you okay?" Callan asks when he reaches us. Kaitlyn comes running over, throws herself into his arms, and he picks her up.

"I think I've been in the sun too long," I tell him and he sets his daughter back down, and puts his arm around me. He leads me to the back of the truck, and I welcome the shade. I sit on the bumper and he grabs me a bottle of water. Kaitlyn dashes off to be with her friends as Callan drops to his knees. Going into professional mode, his gaze moves over my face.

"I'm fine," I tell him, and put one hand on his shoulder. "You don't have to go all first responder on me. It's the sun and I didn't eat properly this morning. I'm sure my blood sugar is just low."

He stares at me like he's not convinced. "Fine, but you need to take it easy tonight. You've been working overtime getting this float ready."

I smile and take in the kids. "Looks good though, doesn't it? We all had so much fun doing it."

"Looks great," he says, but he's not looking at the float, he's looking at me. He leans in and drops a kiss onto my mouth.

"Get a room already," Mason says as he walks by. Just the other day we took Kaitlyn to Mason's house, and the kids played while I got caught up with him and his wife Lisa. I like them both. A lot.

"Go fu—" Callan stops himself when he realizes there are

little ones around. He stands and pulls me to my feet, once again the world spins around me.

His brow furrows as he looks down at me. "Are you sure you're okay?"

"I'm perfectly fine," I inform him, even though it might be a small lie. We promised to be honest with each other, but for the last couple of days I haven't been myself. Maybe Callan is right. Maybe I've been working too hard. "I'll rest tonight. Oh, wait, we have to go to the fireworks."

"We can cancel."

"Are you kidding me?" I give a fast shake of my head and wish I hadn't when dizziness once again hits. I hide it and say, "I don't want to disappoint Kaitlyn like that. She's been really looking forward to them."

"You're right." He nods and thinks about it for a moment. "Fine, you can rest tomorrow night."

"Nope, we have to take Amanda and David out to dinner, remember?"

"Right, but we can cancel that."

"I actually really want to go out." I blink up at him with pleading eyes, but there is a part of me that loves his concern. "I'm looking forward to dressing up and eating at a restaurant."

"Are you saying you're tired of my cooking?"

I laugh at that. Nothing about Callan is tiring, and in fact the more time I spend with him, the harder it's going to be to go back to my place when the summer comes to an end. But it must come to an end. My heart sits a little heavy at that truth.

"I love your cooking. I've just been around kids so much I forget what it's like to be an adult."

"You do need a break," he says.

"Spoken like a true single dad." I smile as I glance at all the happy kids getting dressed for the float as an achy need grips my stomach. I think the clock is ticking on my maternal instincts. I swallow, and glance at Callan, wishing he wanted the same things as me, but he doesn't.

Then again, we have been playing house and having fun. Is it possible that he's moved on, able to accept the past and move into the future, one that's filled with a wife and more children? Or am I simply wishing for what I want? Yeah, I'm sure that's probably all this is, and I'd be wise not to get my hopes up.

"Come on," he says, and puts his arm around me. He walks to a vendor selling drinks and gets me an orange juice. My heart wobbles at his sweetness. "Drink this and go sit there while I get the float hooked up to the truck." I sip my juice and do as he says. But I get antsy sitting, so I jump to my feet, and gather up the kids and we all finish our costumes. As I look at all the kids dressed as nature's animals, I help them onto the float. Soon enough, we're moving along, and we're tossing candy into the crowd.

We all smile and wave, but my smile dies a quick death when I spot Brad. He's standing there in his casual clothes, his gaze latched on me. My heart stalls at the strange look on his face, and I falter a little.

"You okay, Gemma?" Kaitlyn asks.

"Fine, sweetie. Just the movement made me a bit dizzy."

The truck pulls us along, and I think we've lost Brad until I see him moving through the crowd, following us. What the heck is he doing? I catch his eye again, and he crosses his arms and stops. I haven't heard from him since we visited my parents. A few times I thought I spotted him on the street, but in the end, I simply chalked it up to worry. I'm pretty sure he got the hint when Callan and I presented a united front. So why the heck is he here now? It has to be a coincidence. Nothing else makes sense. Right?

I briefly close my eyes to pull myself together and reach

into the basket to toss out more candy to the crowd. I push Brad from my thoughts and brush it off as nothing more than a fluke meeting. Lots of people are out in the crowd watching the parade. That's what people do at parades.

When the parade comes to an end, and all the candy is gone, I help the kids from the float, and wait for their parents to come collect them for the barbecue the firefighters are putting on. I shade the sun from my eyes, still a little spooked at the way Brad was smirking at me, when all of a sudden someone grabs me from behind. I scream, like actually scream, and all eyes turn my way.

"Whoa," Callan says, "I didn't mean to frighten you," he says, his voice deep and reassuring. He turns me, and his gaze narrows. "You look like you've seen a ghost." He looks past my shoulders. "What's going on, Gemma?"

"Nothing really. I saw Brad in the crowd."

He stiffens. "Did he say something? Do something?"

"No. It was just strange seeing him, I guess." I inhale when the scent of food reaches my nose, but instead of teasing my appetite, it makes me feel a bit nauseous. "Let's eat. I'm starving," I say, wanting to change the subject, even though I'm unable to dispel the twisted, angry smirk on Brad's face.

Callan hesitates for a second, but when Kaitlyn comes bounding over, grabbing both our hands so we can swing her, he relaxes. We grab a couple of hot dogs and find a seat at the table. I nibble on mine. I don't want Callan to think anything is wrong, even though seeing Brad again has really thrown me off. I changed my number again after the family gathering, and I've not been back to my small townhouse in ages. Is it possible that he's been looking for me? As a police officer, he'd have no trouble finding out where Callan lives.

That thought gives me pause, and a huge stomachache. Surely to God, Callan and Kaitlyn aren't in any danger, right? Brad has a temper, but he never laid a hand on me before. He might not have left any physical evidence of his abuse. But there was abuse. Still, I don't think he'd go after Callan.

"Gemma," Callan says. "What's wrong?"

"I don't know," I say quietly. No sense in hiding this or trying to change the subject again. Callan can read me like an open book. "I guess...it was weird seeing Brad."

"Weird how?"

"I don't know. The way he looked at me seemed almost... threatening." His jaw clenches with an audible click. "I'm sure it's nothing, though. Maybe I'm just imagining things."

"How about I have a talk with him? Find out what he's really up to."

I give a fast shake of my head. "No, I am not dragging you into this."

"I'm already in it, Gemma," he says.

I take a big breath. "I'll call Mom and Dad later. Just see if he's been coming around, or asking about me."

"Okay," he says, even though he doesn't seem satisfied by that suggestion.

I take a big bite of my hot dog, chew it and force it down. I follow it by a big drink of soda, the carbonation actually helping a bit to settle my stomach.

"Daddy, can we have ice cream?" Kaitlyn asks.

"Of course," he says, and pushes from the bench. We both take Kaitlyn's hands like it's the most natural thing in the world, like we're a little family, and head over to the table where they're scooping out big cones for the kids.

Mason comes up to us. "After the fireworks, the guys are headed to shoot some pool, why don't you come along?"

Callan briefly hesitates, and I nudge him. "Go ahead." Honestly, it's been so long since he's been out with his friends, I sort of feel guilty for hogging all his attention. "I'll take Kaitlyn home after the fireworks, and get her ready for bed. We could use some girl time anyway."

"You sure?" he asks.

"Unless you'd rather her paint your nails tonight."

He grins, and makes a move to kiss me when he remembers Kaitlyn is standing there staring up at us.

"Are you going to be my mommy?" she asks, and as Callan and I go still, Mason gives a low, slow whistle and slaps Callan on the back.

"On that note...I'll see you tonight, bud," he says and walks away.

Callan opens his mouth and closes it, clearly not knowing how to answer so I come to his rescue. One thing is for certain, the shock of her suggestion—written all over his face —is a good indication that me being his daughter's mommy is something he's not interested in.

"No, Kaitlyn," I say, and swallow against the rawness in my throat, because when it comes right down to it, I would love to be a permanent member of this family. But Callan is not interested in a wife, or more children. "We're just friends."

She thinks about that for a second. "All my friends have a mommy. Why can't I?"

Callan puts his hands on her shoulders. "Your mommy—"

"I know she's in heaven," she says. "But Gemma can be my stepmother."

"What do you know about stepmothers?" Callan asks.

"Brooklyn has a stepmother. She doesn't like her, though. She's a mean stepmother." Kaitlyn glances up at me. "She's not nice like you."

"I'm glad you think I'm nice." I tap her nose and note how shaky my finger is. "I think you're nice, too."

"Then you can be my stepmother," she says, like the matter is simple, when it's anything but.

Callan rakes his hand through his hair and glances up at me, an apology in his eyes.

"It's fine," I say my voice low for his ears only. Maybe Callan and I shouldn't be playing house. Maybe this was a bad idea, for so many reasons. Maybe I should put an end to this now, before I too am asking for more, for something he can't give. "Kids her age go through phases. She'll probably forget by tomorrow."

"You think?"

I nod. "Come on." I swing Kaitlyn's arm. "Let's head back and check on Gilbert the guinea pig before we get changed for the fireworks."

"I love Gilbert," Kaitlyn says and hugs her free arm to her chest and rocks. "He's so snuggly."

We make our way to a side street where Callan parked his car, and we all climb in. Kaitlyn talks nonstop on the way home and Callan shakes his head.

"Too much sugar," he says.

"I see I've been a good influence on her," I tease and he reaches across the seat, takes my hand and gives it a squeeze.

"You have been," he says and looks straight ahead, like he has something on his mind.

"I'm glad you're going out with the guys tonight," I tell him.

"Why's that?" he asks, sounding distracted.

"I've been monopolizing all your time. It will be good for you to get out."

We pull into his driveway and he scrubs his face. His thoughts are clearly elsewhere. "Yeah, I guess," he says and unbuckles.

Kaitlyn jumps from the backseat and makes a beeline for the front door. We follow her up and my stomach is tight. What does Callan have on his mind? After his daughter asking if I was going to be her mother, is he thinking maybe we need to end this? Maybe we shouldn't be setting Kaitlyn up for disappointment...maybe I shouldn't be setting myself up for it.

Dammit. Dammit. Dammit.

My heart is a little heavy as we head inside and change into long pants and we all grab sweaters. The air gets much cooler at night, even in the summer. I plaster on a smile, not wanting Callan to think there is anything wrong as we all pile back into his car.

A short while later, we find a grassy spot at the park, which is filled with people, and we settle in to watch the show. Kaitlyn is so hyped, she's running circles around us, but then stops abruptly.

"Daddy, I have to go to the bathroom."

"I can take her," I say and glance at the line near the portables.

"Nah, it's okay. I'll take her. Come on, kiddo. Let's hurry before the show starts." Callan jumps up, and the sun slips lower on the horizon when he disappears into the crowd. I dig into my purse and pull out my phone, about to text Amanda, to make sure we're still on for dinner tomorrow night.

As I text, Callan drops back down next to me. "That was fast," I say but my heart leaps into my throat when I turn and find Brad sitting next to me. He tugs his legs up and wraps his arms around them. "What are you doing here?" I ask and glance around.

He gestures with a nod to the portables. "Lover boy is in the line," he says. "It's just you and me." He eyes me for a second. "Relax, Gemma."

My heart crashes against my chest. "What do you want?"

He shuffles closer and I move from the blanket to the grass. "You know what I want."

"And you know I'm with Callan," I say. "Didn't we make that clear at the weekend gathering?"

"You're not really with him, Gemma." He snorts. "I know all about his wife, and how she died, and how he's not interested in doing that all over again, so believe me when I say I know you're not really with him."

"I don't know where you got your information. But you're wrong," I say, even though it's a lie. Brad is telling me the hard truth that I haven't wanted to face as we played house this last month. "You should leave."

"No, Gemma, you're the one who should leave. If you think he's going to give you what you want, you're wrong."

"You don't know anything about us."

"Now that's where you're wrong. I know everything." I open my mouth to tell him to leave, but he cuts me off. "You always wanted a family, and children of your own. He's not going to give you that, Gemma." A fast pause and then, "I will, though. We used to talk about that, remember?"

Tears fill my eyes, and I work to blink them back. "I remember a lot of things, Brad, and most of them aren't good."

"Things will be different this time."

"You said that to me many times to get me back, but things never changed, Brad. You have anger issues and need therapy."

"That's because you continued to do things that angered me, baby. If you would just stop that..."

I shake my head. Just like a typical narcissist, he's turning the blame on me. Gaslighting me. But I'm stronger now. Being with Callan, a man who treats me with respect, has taught me so much, about myself, and life. I hate that I stayed with him as long as I did, that I believed he would change, that he cared about me enough to try. I was broken then. But I'm not now. Callan helped put the pieces of myself back together.

"We were good," he says in a low soft voice, the same one he used to use when he swore things would get better. But I'm not that girl he once knew. I'm a different person now, and it's not going to work. "Remember how much fun we had when we went to that bed and breakfast on the lake last year?"

"I remember," I say. "Things were good at first, then you got angry when I nearly tipped the canoe. Do you remember that, Brad?"

He ignores the comment and says, "We made love by the fire that night. Remember how good that was?"

I shake my head as my blood rushes faster through my veins, and once again, the world spins around me. I calm myself as my mind goes back to that weekend, and what I remember—Brad taking me rough, getting off and rolling over and going to sleep.

"Just leave, please," I say and inject authority into my voice.

His voice takes on a hard edge when he says, "You'll be mine again, Gemma. I promise you that."

"I don't want you, Brad. I want Callan, and you'll never be half the man he is."

His twisted smirk slithers down my spine and elicits a hard shiver. "Yeah, but he'll never really be yours, now will he? The sooner you realize that, the sooner you'll come back to me."

"No—"

"Don't make this hard on yourself, Gemma. Don't make me come for you."

14

CALLAN

As the morning sun rises on the horizon, I lay in bed, my arm on my forehead as my thoughts go back to yesterday. Jesus, my heart nearly jumped from my chest after Kaitlyn asked if Gemma could be her mother. We've been having fun together and she's so good with my daughter, but committing and giving myself fully, scares the living shit out of me. I can't imagine a life without Gemma in it. But I don't know if I can give her what she wants. After losing a wife and unborn son, I'm not sure I have it in me to walk that road again. Take those kinds of chances.

Last night, on my way back from the portables with Kaitlyn, I knew Gemma and I needed to talk, but realized it would have to wait when I found a very shaken up Gemma. The second she told me about Brad showing up, I jumped up and searched the crowd—even though she didn't want me to. But I was ready to introduce his face to my fist. Just like a fucking bully, he showed up when she was alone. The guy needs to come pick on someone his own size. She insisted she was okay, and that I should go out and shoot pool with the guys, but no way was I leaving her alone.

"Good morning," I say as Gemma rolls over in the bed and opens her eyes. Her smile is warm and enticing, but then it falls. Every muscle in my body tenses. "What's wrong?"

"I...don't know," she says, and jumps from the bed. She hurries into the bathroom and I hear her retching into the toilet. I tug on a pair of sweats and follow her in. She whimpers and waves me off. "Go, I don't want you to see me like this."

"Stop it," I say and take her hair, pulling it back so she doesn't get it wet.

"Callan," she moans. "Ugh, I don't think I should have eaten all that junk yesterday."

I touch her head, and find her a bit warm. "I'm not sure it was the food. You feel a bit feverish, really."

"No," she said. "I don't want to be sick."

"No one does," I say and get her a glass of water. She rinses her mouth and leans against the tub. "Better."

"I think so."

"Think we should get you to the doctor?"

"No, it's probably something I ate..." She goes quiet, and frowns.

"Or maybe it's because of Brad," I say. "I think we need to go to the police, Gemma. This could be the result of stress."

"I don't want to. I want this to just go away."

"I don't think he's going away." I push her damp hair from her forehead. "He threatened you."

"Callan, if anything ever happened to you and Kaitlyn because—"

"Nothing is going to happen to us," I tell her. "Or you. You're staying with me, in this house until he's out of your life for good."

"I'm not sure that's ever going to happen. His parents are best friends with my parents, remember, and I'm only here for a little while longer. I need to get back to my place, and to my real life before the new school year starts. You won't need me here then. Kaitlyn won't need a nanny."

I open my mouth, wanting to tell her I do need her, and her being here with me isn't just to take care of Kaitlyn. I want her here with me, but how can I say those things when I'm not sure I can give her what she needs? I'm not going to be the guy to keep her from having a house full of children, because I'm too much of a chicken shit, too afraid of loving and losing...again. Even if I wasn't afraid, I can't forget the reminder she just gave me—she needs to get back to her real life. Yeah, I get it, this one is just pretend. Although, I'm not even sure we're pretending anymore. Or is she just not feeling what I'm feeling?

Fuck me.

She looks down, her brow furrowed, and I worry she's going to be sick again.

"Gemma, what's wrong?"

We both turn at the sound of Kaitlyn's voice.

"I'm not feeling well," Gemma says.

Kaitlyn opens the sliver of a closet, takes out a cloth and runs it under the water. She puts it on Gemma's forehead and my heart swells.

"This is what Daddy does when I don't feel good."

"Thank you, sweetie," Gemma says. "I'm sorry I woke you. Why don't you go back to bed? You don't want to be tired when you go visit your grandparents later."

"You didn't wake me. There was a noise outside. A big bang."

Gemma and I both look at each other, and from the widening of her eyes, it's clear we're both thinking the same thing. "Kaitlyn, go crawl into bed with Gemma. I'm going to check things out."

Gemma captures my arm. "Callan. Please, don't."

I put my hand on hers. "I'm sure it's nothing, but you two go jump in bed, okay?"

She nods and I help her to her feet. When they're both under the blankets, I tug on a T-shirt and head outside.

I walk the house and find the garbage can tipped over. I fix it and head back inside. The girls are talking quietly when I reach the bedroom.

"I think it was a racoon. The garbage was tipped."

Kaitlyn laughs, clearly finding the idea funny. "Come on, kiddo. You need a few more hours of sleep. So does Gemma."

Kaitlyn gives Gemma a kiss on the cheek. "I hope you feel better."

"I already do," she says, her lids falling shut before I can even get Kaitlyn out the door. I get Kaitlyn tucked in and go back in to check on Gemma, who is fast asleep. I touch her forehead again and find her still a bit warm.

I make my way to the kitchen and put on a pot of coffee, a little too worked up to fall back to sleep. Cup of java in hand, I head to the garage to do a bit of tidying, all the while thinking I should call the cops and get a restraining order against Brad. Gemma doesn't want me to, but him showing up last night and threatening her...well, he needs to know he can't get away with shit like that.

I work out my frustrations by cleaning, and when I check the time, it's eight, time for Kaitlyn to get up and head to her grandparents. Although maybe I'll keep her here. If Gemma isn't well, we won't be going out to dinner tonight.

I head back inside, and Kaitlyn is in the bathroom when I reach the top step. "Almost done, Daddy," she calls out and I stick my head into my bedroom. Gemma opens one eye, and smiles at me.

I cross the room and sit on the bed. "How are you feeling?"

"So much better. I'm not sure what that was all about but it's passed, and I'm actually starving."

I chuckle and tug the blankets down. "I'll make us breakfast." I pause. "Do you still want to go out tonight, or do you want to just stay in and rest?"

She looks past my shoulder to see if the coast is clear, grabs my T-shirt and brings me close, her mood very different from earlier this morning. "I want to go out to dinner, and then I want to come back here. But not to rest."

I laugh. "What's gotten into you?"

"Tonight, it will be you," she teases, and I put my hand on her cheek.

"I'm not so sure that's a good idea. You're still flushed."

"Yeah, but it's not because I'm sick," she says, a smile on her face.

"Well enough to help with breakfast."

"Burnt toast and runny eggs coming up."

I laugh. "On that note." I stand, and say, "I'll get started. Come down when you're ready." I head downstairs and find Kaitlyn in front of the TV. "Want to help me with breakfast?"

"Can we have pancakes with the smiley face?"

"Sure," I say and she jumps up.

"I'll get the chocolate chips."

I roll my eyes. She never thought to put chocolate chips in her pancakes until Gemma taught her and turned it into something fun by making them into a smiley face. Kaitlyn loves them, but I only let her have the chocolate on the weekends and as a special treat.

She grabs the bag, and I reach for the bowl. "Daddy, I want a baby brother," she says, and I nearly choke on my tongue.

"You do, huh?" I say quickly pulling myself together.

"Baily just got a baby brother. Can I have one too?"

"Well, kiddo, it's not really that easy."

"I know you need a mommy to have a baby, but Gemma is going to be my mommy, right?"

Well fuck. So much for her forgetting about that.

I pull a chair out and gesture for her to sit. I drop into the one next to her. "Where is all this coming from?" I ask, my throat so goddamn tight it's a bit hard to talk.

"I want a real mommy," she says with a frown, her eyes big and sad. My gut clenches. "And I want a baby brother to play with."

"I know you do, honey," I say, hating that I've deprived her of this. "But I don't think that's something that's going to happen. We got Gilbert for you to play with."

She folds her arms and her eyes fill with tears. My fucking heart nearly splits into two. "It's not the same."

"I know," I say and ruffle her hair. "But we can't have a baby without a mommy, right?"

"But Gemma can be our mommy."

I tug on my hair, not knowing how to handle this. "Honey, a man and a woman must love each other before they get married and make a baby."

"Do you love Gemma?"

A noise behind me has me jumping to my feet, and when I find Gemma standing there, her eyes big, I figure she heard most of our conversation.

"Let's get at those pancakes," I say. "Then we need to get you to your grandparents."

I step around the island and busy myself as Gemma slowly enters the kitchen, like she's unsure whether she should be here or not.

"Gemma, are you feeling better?" Kaitlyn asks.

"I am," she says and gives her a tap on the nose. "Thank you for asking, Kaitlyn." She nods to the cage on the table in the corner. "How is Gilbert today?"

Her mouth opens, like she just had an epiphany. "Daddy,

can we get a girl guinea pig and they can get married and have babies?"

"Ah, we'll see," I say before I can think better of it, and Kaitlyn jumps up and down and starts clapping. My eyes seek Gemma's and she's cringing. She comes my way and stands beside me as Kaitlyn takes Gilbert from the cage.

"What have you done?" she whispers.

"I don't know. All this talk about a baby brother has rattled me."

"Yeah, I heard that. I didn't mean to listen in. Pretty deep conversation for an early Saturday morning."

"I don't think I handled it very well."

"You did perfectly fine," she says. "You have to be honest with her, Callan. If more children aren't in your future, it's best she knows that. She's a kid, she's resilient, and not having a sibling will in no way hurt her."

I nod, even though I'm not a hundred percent sure about that. Gemma pours a cup of coffee and takes a sip. She makes a face, like she'd just tasted something spoiled.

"What's wrong?"

"Tastes funny," she says. I take the cup from her and take a drink. Seems okay to me. "I can make a fresh pot. This one has been on a long time."

"I can do it," she says and as she turns her attention to the coffee, and I glance at my daughter, who is telling Gilbert all about his upcoming wedding, and how he's going to be a daddy soon.

My phone rings and I pull it from my pocket to read a message from Mason. The guys were disappointed that I stayed in last night, but after Gemma's run in with Brad, I wasn't going anywhere.

Mason: Hey bud, what's up?

Callan: Getting breakfast and Kaitlyn ready to go to her grandparents.

Mason: Is Gemma going to be Kaitlyn's new mommy!!!

I roll my eyes at the message.

Callan: Very funny.

Mason: Actually, I'm being serious.

I stare at the phone. How the hell do I reply to that? Three dots appear and I wait for his next message.

Mason: You two are good together, bud. Maybe you want to think about that.

Callan: It's not like that.

Mason. Then make it like that.

I set my phone down as my heart jumps into my throat for the umpteenth time this morning. I turn to find Gemma staring at me.

"Everything okay?" she asks, and glances at my phone, worry lingering in her eyes.

"It was just Mason."

"He must be disappointed that you didn't go out last night."

"He's fine," I say and pour water into the package batter.

Her eyes narrow, unconvinced. "Is he giving you a hard time about something? You look upset."

I think about that for a second. I've told Gemma numerous times I didn't want any more children—heck, Kaitlyn is all I can handle, or at least I thought so. While Gemma is adamant that Kaitlyn will be okay if we maintain the same life, as I look at my daughter, something deep inside me shifts, and all the hollowed-out spots fill with warmth and hope for a future. My God, what is happening to me? My heart beats a little faster as I envision Kaitlyn cooing over a new baby, but the biggest part of that picture is the woman holding the child—Gemma.

Is it possible that I can give Gemma everything she wants? Does she even want everything from me? I'm not sure but what I do know right now is we're going to have to talk...

and soon. But first I have to get my daughter ready, and Gemma and I have a dinner date. Talking will have to wait, but that doesn't mean I can't show her how much I care, how well we fit together, in other ways.

15

GEMMA

"You look gorgeous," Callan says when he enters the bedroom and finds me all dressed up and slipping on a pair of my favorite white gold earrings, a graduation present from my parents. I glance at him in the mirror, and take in his dress shirt, tie and pants. I sigh, my body warming at the mere sight of him. How will I ever be with another man, or even find one attractive after spending time with Callan? The simple answer is this. I won't. Honest to God, who knew I'd fall so hard for him. Then again, how could a girl not? The way he makes me feel about myself, the way he's looking at me this very second, like I'm the most important woman in the world, well, that can really do a number on a girl's head—make them think there is more going on when there isn't.

"You clean up pretty nice yourself," I say, and he slides his arms around me, pulling my back to his chest. He puts his mouth on my neck and makes a growling sound that vibrates through me and stimulates all my erogenous zones as he kisses me. I'm not one-hundred percent sure what's going on with him. After exchanging messages with Mason this morning, he seemed upset, maybe even a little spooked, but then his mood shifted, changed...became lighter, like the weight of the world had come off his shoulders. I have no idea what Mason said, but I'm happy to see Callan smiling.

Truthfully, I feel that lightness myself, especially after giving myself a good hard lecture over breakfast this morning. Callan and I don't want the same things, and we don't have a future together. I've come to accept that fact, and have since decided to enjoy the rest of the summer with him and when it's over, it's over. I'm simply going to enjoy it while I can and deal with my feelings when all is said and done. Brad might be a complete jerk, but he was right. Callan will never get over past hurts and move on, and the sooner I accept it, the better it will be for my head and my stupid heart. Who am I kidding? My heart will never heal after Callan.

"Keep that up and we'll never get out of here," I say as he slides his hands down my sides and grips my hips. I lean back, pressing against his growing erection, and he moans. The sweet sound vibrates through me, settles deep between my legs.

"We don't have to go," he says. "We could stay here instead, and I can ravish you."

"Yes, we do. I've been looking forward to getting out with my sister, and enjoying a nice meal."

"Yeah, me too actually." He steps back and I grin as he adjusts his pants.

"We can take care of that little problem later," I say.

He grins at my use of the word little and checks his watch. "We better get going."

He puts his hand on the small of my back and leads me downstairs. I relax into the passenger seat as he backs out onto the road. I'm glad whatever illness I had this morning is long gone. I really am looking forward to spending time with Amanda, even if she is a troublemaker.

Callan reaches across the seat and takes my hand in his. He gives it a squeeze, the way he's done so many times before, and it wraps around my heart. My throat tightens, but I smile, not wanting him to know how much I've fallen for him. My God, when this started, we were both so sure what we wanted, and what we didn't. Things have changed drastically for me, but he's not giving me any indication that they've changed for him.

I reach for the radio and turn it up, wanting to drown out the sound of my heart crashing against my ribs. I hum along as he drives and less than fifteen minutes later, we reach the seafood restaurant Amanda picked. Inside, Callan gives his name, but I spot Amanda and David waving us over. I follow the hostess and she seats us across from them.

"Hey guys," I say, greeting Amanda and David as I set my purse on the back of my chair.

"Wow, you two look great," Amanda says and I grin at her.

"Thanks. It was nice to get out of sweats for a change."

Amanda laughs and nudges David. "Hear that?" she teases.

"What's so funny?"

"I thought you two would still be in the honeymoon stage, not the sweatpants stage. That's for old married couples like us."

"Hey, I take offence to that," David says.

We all laugh at that. "I'm around kids all day too, and we have Kaitlyn at night."

"Oh right, I forgot my little sister is all domesticated now." She opens the wine menu, but her gaze is riveted on me. I touch my mouth. Did I smear my lipstick or something? As David and Callan talk about the big fire two weeks ago, I eye my sister.

"Why are you staring at me?"

"I don't know." She purses her lips in thought. "There's something different about you."

"Different good or different bad?"

"Good. Definitely good." She reaches across the table and takes my hand. "It's just so nice to see you happy again." My thoughts instantly go to Brad and his threat, and my sister is far too good at reading me. "What?"

"I ran into Brad at the fireworks last night," I say, my voice low.

"More like he stalked her," Callan pipes in.

Amanda's eyes go wide. "Are you serious? Why is he still bothering you?"

"Because he's an asshole," Callan says and puts a protective arm around my shoulder. "Don't worry, though. I don't plan to let her out of my sight for a minute."

"Maybe you should talk to Mom and Dad." Amanda toys with her napkin and continues with, "Maybe they could talk to his parents or something. He shouldn't be stalking you, Gemma. I never liked the way he always seemed controlling with you, but that's a bit scary."

I hold my hands up, palms out. "I'm not dragging Mom and Dad into my problems, and potentially ruin their relationship with their best friends, and honestly, the last person I want to talk about tonight is Brad."

"Yeah, you're right," Amanda says. "Now let me have a look at that wine list." She winks at us. "Since we beat your sorry asses and the bill is on you two tonight..."

I laugh at that as the server comes over to take our drink orders. Amanda picks a nice bottle of wine for the table and we open our food menus. My stomach takes that moment to growl and I chuckle.

"I haven't eaten since breakfast," I say. After pancakes, I lost my appetite again, but it's back full force now.

"When have you ever missed a meal?" Amanda teases.

"She wasn't feeling great," Callan says. "I think it might have been the candy apple followed by the cotton candy."

"That'll do it," David says with a chuckle. "You always were one for sweets, Gemma."

The waiter returns with bread and with little finesse, I dive in, eating like I've been lost in the desert and living off rations.

We fall into easy conversation and soon enough our meals are served. I smile. I love being out with my sister like this. Love spending couples time together. My stomach squeezes tight. Soon enough this is going to come to an end too.

Stop!

I refuse to let those unhappy thoughts infiltrate my brain tonight. I just want to enjoy the time I have left with Callan and not ruin it with thoughts that sadden me. I take a sip of my wine, and for some unknown reason tears prick my eyes. What the hell is wrong with me? I guess I can try to pretend a future without him won't bother me, but deep inside, I'm an emotional mess.

I twist my napkin between my hands, and try to think happy thoughts when the server returns to clear our plates and take our dessert orders. My sister is watching me carefully when I place my napkin on the table and force a smile

"I have to go to the little girl's room," I say.

"I'll join you," Amanda says. "I need to freshen up my lipstick."

Our heels click as we make our way through the restaurant, and once we're inside the ladies' room Amanda puts her hands on my shoulders.

"What's wrong?" she asks. "You looked like you were about to cry at least ten times tonight."

"I don't know. I'm a bit of an emotional mess," I say. I take in her big blue eyes and consider telling her that my relationship with Callan is a fake one, even though it feels far too real to me.

"Gemma."

"Yeah?" I ask when she goes all serious on me.

"When was the last time you had a period?"

I go perfectly still, my mind racing, working to count down the days. "I...my God, I've been so busy, I totally lost track. Wait, okay, two weeks ago, I spotted. I didn't have a full period, but I chalked that up to my crazy busy schedule, and hormones from all the sex I've been having."

"Lucky girl, but do you think..."

"Oh, my God, no!" My words come out in a hushed whisper as I back up until I hit the wall. I lean forward, brace my hands on my knees, and take deep gulping breaths. "I can't be."

"Actually, you can be. You've been having a lot of sex."

I shake my head and my hair falls over my face. "We used a condom at first, but then stopped because I'm on the pill. I mean, I might have forgotten a pill or two, but still. I mean both you and Nicole tried for months and months to get pregnant."

"That doesn't mean it will be the same for you, and it only takes once, you know?"

"I know," I shoot back, angrier than I should be. Dammit, what is wrong with me? "I'm sorry."

"It's okay. Your hormones are all over the place." I stand up right and smooth my hair back. With a rejuvenating breath I step to the sink and splash cold water on my face. Once done, I catch Amanda's eyes in the mirror. "You said you were sick this morning. Do you think it could have been morning sickness?"

"I don't know," I say, and put my hand over my stomach. "This can't be happening." I turn to face Amanda, my hands behind me, gripping the sink.

"I know this is a shock, Gemma. But you and Callan, you two are so right for each other. Isn't marriage and children the next step?"

I shake my head hard. "No, it's not. None of this is what you think."

She takes a step closer, her voice low when she asks, "What's going on?"

"Callan and I *are* good together. You were right when you said that, and your first instincts were right, too. We were pretending. He was helping me send a message to Brad. We exercised relationship rights, thinking it couldn't hurt anything."

"Oh no." She pulls me in for a hug. I lay my head on her shoulder. "You love him, don't you?"

I nod and sniffle. "We were only going to be together for the summer. I fell in love with him and screwed everything up. And now this...I could be pregnant."

"You didn't do it alone. Maybe his feelings for you have changed. I see the way he looks at you, Gemma."

My heart jumps. "He doesn't want kids. Even if he wanted me, he made it clear he didn't want kids. He's not going to be happy about this. Not one little bit."

"Okay," she says in her best calming, big sister voice. "Before you get yourself all worked up, we have to find out if you really are pregnant."

I swipe at the tears. "I need a test."

"Yes, you do," she says and grabs a piece of paper towel to dab the corners of my eyes.

"I'll pick one up tomorrow," I say.

"Do you want to continue with tonight? I can say I'm not feeling well, and we can get out of here."

I give her a fast, grateful hug. I'm so glad she's here with me tonight. "No, we'll eat our desserts," I say. "There's nothing I can do tonight. This will have to wait until tomorrow."

"I can come over, be there when you take it."

I give a fast shake of my head. "No, that will raise suspicions. I'll go to my townhouse for privacy. I'll make an excuse. Say I need to pick something up."

"Tell him we're going shopping or something."

"Yeah, that will work," I say, even though I don't like to lie, this fib is necessary. If I'm not pregnant, everything will be fine. If I am, I'm going to need my sister by my side to help me figure out what to do next. I take a deep breath to pull myself together. "We should get back out there."

She nods and I follow her back to our table. I put on a smile, and while David and Callan are in deep conversation, his brow furrows when he looks at me.

When the conversation ends, he leans in. "You feeling okay?"

"Just tired," I say.

"You've been working too hard, taking care of all the kids at the club, and Kaitlyn at nights. Tonight, when we get home, I'm going to take care of you," he says quietly.

"Okay," I say, liking the sound of that.

We eat our desserts, sip our coffee, and soon enough the night comes to an end. Callan pays the bill and we all stand to say goodbye. I give Amanda a big hug as the guys shake hands.

"Don't forget about tomorrow," she says, and I nearly swallow my damn tongue.

"What's going on tomorrow?" David asks.

"Gemma and I are going shopping."

"Glad to hear it," Callan says. "She needs a break."

"I'll call you tomorrow," I say to her, and fall into step with Callan as he leads me outside to his car. He casts me a quick glance.

"That was fun. We should do that more often," he says. "I really like Amanda and David."

"They are fun," I say, and blink to keep the tears at bay. My God, if I am pregnant, is Callan going to think I did it on purpose? Is he going to hate me? He's definitely not the kind of guy to shirk his responsibilities, so he'll take responsibility, but that in no way means I come with the package. I'm so lost in my thoughts and worries, I'm sure he must be picking up on it. I turn to take in the firm lines in his profile, but he too seems to be a little lost in his own thoughts.

We sit in silence until he pulls into his driveway, and he comes around my side when I step from the car. His mouth turns up, his eyes full of playfulness as he tugs me to him.

"As much as I like you in this dress, Gemma. I really, really want you out of it."

"I want that too," I say as tears pound against my eyes. I'm a hot mess of emotions and I can't seem to get control over them. We hurry inside and with Kaitlyn gone for the weekend, Callan releases the zipper on my dress and tugs it down to my feet. He gives a low whistle as I stand before him in nothing but lacy bra and panties.

"God, you are so gorgeous."

"And you're overdressed," I tease, waving a finger up and down his body.

"When you're right you're right," He says and in that manly way of his, he tugs on his tie, and unbuttons his shirt. No matter how many times I've seen this man naked, I'm still like a kid in a candy store. He tugs off his pants and scoops me up. His mouth finds mine, and I expect him to lead me to his room but there's a new kind of hunger in him, an eagerness that leads us to the chair in the living room.

"Bedroom. Too far," he says, all caveman-like as he sits in the chair and pulls me onto his lap. His hard cock presses against my center, and I squirm, needing him inside me. I'm not sure what tomorrow or the future brings, but tonight... tonight he's mine and this might be the very last time he is, so I'm going to enjoy everything between us.

CALLAN

I roll over in bed, and sit upright when I find the other side empty. I scratch my face, and glance around the room. My vision is blurry, but it's not much wonder. We were up half the night making love.

Making love?

Hell yeah, that's what we were doing. No one can kiss and touch me like Gemma did, if she didn't have deeper feelings. I should have talked to her before we fell asleep. I should have straight out told her what she meant to me, but her lids fell shut and I figured we had today.

But now, as I sit here in bed, trying to get my brain to work, I have the strangest feeling that I might be too late. "Gemma," I call out, but when my words aren't met with an answer, I kick the covers off and go for my phone. I'm about to text her when I remember that she was going shopping with her sister. It is late morning, so she probably let me sleep in while she slipped out.

Worry leaves my gut, and a smile I have no control over tugs at my mouth. Tonight, I'm going to tell Gemma how I feel, and pray to fucking God she wants what I want. The thoughts of bringing another child into this world, of making a commitment to Gemma, don't scare me like they used to.

I take a shower, eat breakfast, and tidy up a bit. I'm spending a few hours in the garage when my phone pings. My heart jumps, and I laugh. Yeah, I'm batshit crazy about the girl, but disappointment sits heavy when I see it's Mason. I slide my finger across the phone.

"Hey."

"Jeez, don't be so happy to hear from me."

I laugh. "I just thought you were Gemma."

"Big difference, bro. You free?"

"I am."

"Good, come on over and shoot some pool with us."

"Sounds like a great plan. Be there shortly." I end the call and shoot a text off to Gemma. I wait a few minutes and when no response comes, I chalk it up to her being with her sister, or maybe she misplaced her phone again. She seems to do that a lot.

I tuck my phone into my back pocket, hop into my car and make my way to Burgers and Brews. A few of the guys are already inside, shooting the shit while they shoot a game of pool.

"Hey, look what the cat dragged in," Jack says.

"Funny."

"Gemma let you out, did she?" Colin teases.

"I don't need to ask permission."

"No, he doesn't. He just prefers her company to ours," Mason says as he throws his arm around my shoulder.

"Can't blame him for that," Colin says. "I'm just pissed I didn't get to call first dibs."

A jolt of jealousy races through me. "You," I say and point at Colin. "Keep ten feet away." Colin is a huge player. A different pair of women's panties on his floor every morning. At least that's what I've been told.

"Pussy-whipped," Colin teases.

"One day when you fall for a girl, you'll see what it's like."

The three guys go perfectly still, all eyes trained on me and that's when I realize what I said. "Yeah, I love her, so fuck off."

Laughter breaks out around me, and I get numerous pats on the back. "I'm happy for you, buddy," Mason says. "You deserve someone like Gemma in your life."

"Yeah, you do," Colin says. "But Jesus, what did she ever do to end up with the likes of you? She must have pissed someone off in a past lifetime."

I grab him and put his head in a grip. "Asshole," I say as I rub my knuckles over his head. The waitress comes and clears her throat. "Oh, hey," Tara says. "Keep that up and Jesse will toss your ass out of here."

"Not likely," Mason says. "Not when he finds out our boy here is in love."

A wide smile spreads over Tara's face. She throws her arms around me. "Callan, I'm so happy. I've seen you and Gemma together, and you guys are such a good couple." She glances around. "Is she here?"

"No, she's not, and guys, I haven't even told her that I love her yet and I'm not sure how she feels, so keep it quiet."

They all zip their lips and while I know I can trust them, I'm sure they're bursting to spread the news.

"Don't worry. She loves you too," Tara says.

"How do you know that?"

"Because I'm a woman and I know things." She turns and eyes Colin. "Not a word from the peanut gallery," she warns. "Can I get you a beer, Callan?"

"Yeah. Thanks."

"It's on the house," she says and as she walks away, I check my phone again, hoping to hear from Gemma. I frown.

"Pussy-whipped," Colin teases under his breath and I grab a pool cue.

"Play me. It's been a while since I beat your sorry ass."

I spend the next couple of hours hanging with the guys and for the first time in a very long time, I feel like myself again. I'll always love Zoe. Always. She was my first, my everything, and the mother of our child, and deep in my heart, I know she'd be happy for Gemma and me. She wouldn't want me alone, just like I wouldn't want her alone.

"I'm checking out, guys," I say, after glancing at my phone again.

More pats come on the back. "Good seeing *you*," Mason says, and I know exactly what he means. He hasn't seen the real *me* in a very long time. I head out, make a quick trip to the grocery store so I can make something special for Gemma, and I pick her up some flowers. But as more and more time passes, worry gnaws at my gut.

I grab my phone and call her, but it goes to voice mail. I'm a worrier by nature, especially after Zoe's accident, and not hearing from her all day doesn't sit right. Something must be wrong. I pace around inside my place, going through every worst scenario I can think of. Finally, I look up David and Amanda's number and call.

"Hello," Amanda says, and if nothing is wrong, I don't want to worry her.

"Hey Amanda. Is Gemma still with you?"

A moment of silence and then, "No, ah. She's not."

My stomach tightens, and I don't miss the unease in Amanda's voice. "She's not called you?"

"No, why, did she say she was going to?"

"Um, yeah. She ah...she was going to do some things around her place, so maybe that's all it is."

"She's at her place?"

"Last I knew she was."

I shake my head. What is going on here? Everything in my gut tells me Amanda knows something I don't. "When was the last time you saw her?"

"About thirty minutes ago."

I move toward my door. "I'll head over there."

"Um, maybe it's best that you don't."

My steps slow. "Why wouldn't I?"

"Maybe she...uh, just needs some time to herself. You know, girl time."

I don't believe her for one second. "Yeah, I'm heading over," I say and end the call. I dart outside, hop into my car, and hurry through traffic. My throat is so fucking tight I can barely swallow, and my heart is crashing against my ribs so hard, I'm sure they're going to snap.

I finally reach her place, park my car and head to her door. I stand on the stoop and knock. I wait a second and no answer comes, so I look through the window. A car pulls up behind mine and Amanda steps from it, her face a bit pale.

"What's going on?" I ask.

"Is she not home?" she asks, and worries her lips.

"Where is she, Amanda?" I ask, my voice darker as dread takes hold. Jesus Christ, I need answers and I need them now.

"I have a key." She slides it into the door. I push through and hurry around her place, but she's nowhere to be found. I grip my hair and tug.

"What the fuck?" I say. "Did you guys go shopping?"

"Uh, yeah, sort of," she says. She walks down the hall, steps into the bedroom and opens the closet.

"What are you doing?"

"Just seeing if her things are here."

"Why wouldn't her things be here?" I fight the full-blown panic simmering below the surface.

She takes a few breaths, and it's not hard to tell she's keeping something from me. "Let's go sit down."

"I don't want to sit down. I want you to tell me what's going on."

"I don't want to be the one to tell you this, and I really don't know where Gemma is, and I'm a bit scared, because of her mental state right now."

Every muscle tenses. "Does this have something to do with Brad?"

"Please, let's just sit," she says and walks past me. I follow her to the living room and drop into the chair.

"What?"

She takes a big swallow, and says, "She took a pregnancy test today."

The room closes in on me, sucking the air from my lungs as her words race around my brain. She's on the pill, and we used a condom. Albeit that condom was outdated, and then we stopped using them because she's was on the pill. "Is she pregnant?" I ask, remembering how sick she yesterday morning.

"Don't be mad, Callan," she says and leans forward. "She didn't do it on purpose. She wouldn't do that to you. She was afraid to tell you."

"Why would I think she did it on purpose? Wait, did she say that?" Shit, does she think so little of me. Yeah, sure I said numerous times I wasn't interested in a family or more kids, but come on. Doesn't she know me better than that? But that's not my main focus right now. "Is she pregnant?"

"She's pregnant, Callan, but she wouldn't have run away. I know my sister."

The world closes in on me. My God, I'm going to be a father again, and while I want to take joy in that, at the moment I can't. "Where is she, then?"

"I don't know. She told me she was going to talk to you. None of this makes sense, actually."

I jump to my feet. "She's in trouble."

"Oh, God, she must be." Amanda stands on shaky legs, her eyes big and worried.

Old worries and fears come racing back in a burst. Something is wrong. Every instinct I possess tells me it is. "I can't lose her," I say around the huge lump in my throat. "I can't lose her and our baby."

"You won't," Amanda says and puts her arm on my shoulder, giving me a reassuring squeeze that does little to reassure me.

Fear grips my gut, and I nearly vomit. "It can't happen again. We have to find her. Now."

Amanda nods. "I have an idea."

17

GEMMA

My entire body is shaking as I give my sister a kiss goodbye and shut the door to my townhouse behind her. I drop to the floor and bury my face in my hands. How could this have happened? I never thought forgetting my pill for one night could lead to pregnancy. I put my hand on my stomach. What am I going to do? What would Callan want me to do? He's not the kind of guy to suggest I abort, and the truth is, I don't want one. We made a beautiful baby, and there is a part of me holding out hope that he might want this as much as I do, despite telling me numerous times that he's not interested in a family.

I stare at my phone, and see that he's messaged me. I run my finger over the screen, and consider how the conversation might go down. Amanda was right when she told me the longer I put it off, the harder it will be. I'm just going to have to put on my big girl panties and tell him he's going to be a father again, and hope he wants the mother who's giving birth to his baby.

I take a deep breath, ready to call, when my front door opens. I look up, expecting to see Amanda. Did she forget something? But when my eyes land on Brad, I jump to my feet.

"What are you doing here?" I ask as he closes the door behind him.

"Now that you're back home, does that mean lover boy finally put you out?"

"Brad, what is going—"

"What's going on is we're going to figure out our future."

He steps up to me and his grip on my arm is tight, forceful. I try to tug away, but can't. I take a fast breath and calm myself, as I think about the best way to handle this situation. Getting myself worked up and angering him, has never worked in my favor before.

"You want to talk, then talk," I say.

"Not here."

"Why not here?" I try to appear casual as I say, "It's the perfect spot. We won't get interrupted."

"I just saw your sister leave. Who knows if she'll come back and I'd prefer to go somewhere where we won't be disturbed."

Okay, this is not good. Not good at all.

I hold my phone, and position it in my hand, wanting to dial 911 without him privy to what I'm doing.

"Do you want to pack a bag?" he asks.

"Yeah," I say. If I can get to my room, I can lock the door and call for help.

"I'll be right back." I turn to go to my room, but he's right on my heels, his breath hot on my neck. "What happened with you and the girl you brought to the weekend gathering?"

"We're over," he says. "It's only ever been you I wanted, Gemma."

In my room, I open my closet and reach for my duffle bag, stalling for as long as I can. If Callan doesn't hear from me, maybe he'll come looking, sooner rather than later, because later might just be too late.

Brad sits on my bed, his eyes trained on me. "I told my parents we were getting back together. They were happy for us, Gemma."

I just nod. "Do you want to call your parents and tell them the same?"

"I don't think that's necessary, do you?" I say. "It's Sunday, they love to golf. I don't want to bother their game."

"Call them," he says. "Tell them we're together again."

"Brad—"

"You don't want anyone to worry about you. I mean, if your sister calls and you don't answer, I want her to know you're with me."

"Okay," I say, and lift my phone. My God, I'm clutching it so tightly, my knuckles are white. I pull up their contact and hit call. Brad steps in behind me and puts his arm around my neck in a choke hold. He's not cutting off my air or anything, but it's an aggressive move—a warning.

"Darling, how are you? I was just thinking of you," Mom says when she answers but there is something off in her voice.

"Hey Mom. Sorry to catch you on the golf course."

"We just finished. We're actually having a bite to eat in the club house. Misty and John are with us. They told us you and Brad were back together. I was surprised by the news and that you didn't tell us yourself."

"Yeah, I guess we're all surprised," I say, and Brad tightens his hold. "It happened rather fast."

"Hey Janice," Brad says.

"Oh, you're with him now," Mom says.

"Yeah, he's here at my place," I say, hoping my mother can pick up on my distress and call for help.

"Not for long," Brad says. "We're going to go away for a few days and make up for lost time."

"Where are you going?" Mom asks.

"It's a surprise," Brad says before I can answer.

"Okay," Mom says. "You two have a nice time, and Gemma, call me when you get there."

"I will," I say a measure of relief going through me. If she asked me to call, chances are Brad will want me to. He won't want anyone knowing there could be anything wrong—and there is plenty wrong, that's for sure.

He removes his arm from around my neck. "She seemed happy by the news."

"Yeah, I guess so."

He spins me until I'm facing him. "We're going to be good, Gemma. You wait and see. We'll have that family you always wanted."

Oh, my God. I don't dare tell him I'm pregnant with Callan's baby.

He keeps a good firm hold of my arm as he takes me to his car and stands by the passenger side until I'm buckled in. As he circles, I think about jumping out and running, but he's too fast and too strong and will have me in a second flat. Plus, I'm too frightened to do anything that could put the baby in jeopardy. For the time being, the only thing I can do is play along.

"Where are we going?" I ask and take in the street names as he drives.

He smiles at me. "It's a surprise."

"I don't really like surprises," I say, and take in the clenching of his jaw, the shift in his mood. It's dark, much like the clouds overhead.

"I didn't want to have to come and get you this way, Gemma. You left me no choice."

"Brad," I say. "I was home. I was going to call you."

His head jerks my way. "Really?"

"What you said was right. Things were never going to

work out between Callan and me. He was just a passing phase, you know."

"Don't fuck with me, Gemma. I'll know it."

"I'm not," I say. "You showing up suddenly took me by surprise. I didn't have all my thoughts sorted out. That's all."

"You sorted out now?" he asks.

"I am."

He takes my hand and squeezes it, a gesture Callan has done a hundred times, but this time my heart is in my throat and it's all I can do to fight off the panic. I gently tug my hand back, and dig into my purse, hoping to secretly make a call.

"What are you doing?"

"Chapstick," I say, and pull out the tube. I apply it to my lips and can only hope my sister calls my mother, or Callan gets worried about me.

We drive for what feels like hours, and the sun is low on the horizon when he takes an exit and drives down a long road until numerous cabins on a lake come in to view.

"Where are we?" I ask, and wonder if I'll even have phone service here.

"A little country getaway," he says. "The perfect place for us to reconnect."

Jesus, the man could kill me out here and no one would ever find the body. I grip my seatbelt, not wanting to take it off. He leans over and touches my face. "Relax, baby. We're going to have some fun."

That's what I'm worried about.

I try not to cringe as he touches me. "Have you been here before?" I ask.

"With the guys. We did some fishing."

Okay, well at least someone might know where we are. Not that the 'guys' will come to my rescue here.

"I don't really want to go out on a boat," I say, fear gripping me. He could so easily knock me out and toss me over. Bile punches into my throat, as he exits the car, and as he grabs our bags from the back, I reach for my phone. My hands are shaking so bad, I can barely punch in my code.

I jump when I find him standing beside my window. "What are you doing?"

"I'm going to call Mom, remember she asked me to."

He opens my door, takes my phone from me, and puts it in his pocket. "Why don't we wait on that. Let's go inside, have a drink."

"Okay," I say and step from the car. My shaky legs will barely carry me to the door, and I check for lights on in the other cabins. I spot one three doors down that looks like it could be occupied. If I can make it there...

As though reading my mind, Brad takes hold of my arm and walks me into the cabin. I look around, searching for anything I can use as a weapon if things get ugly, which I'm hoping they don't, but suspecting they will.

He drops our bags into the bedroom, and comes back into the room as I catalogue it.

"You like it?" he asks.

"Yeah, but I think I should call Mom. I don't want her to worry."

"You're with me, what could she possibly be worried about? They adore me, Gemma. You know that."

Right now, in this moment, I'm kicking my ass for not letting my parents know what he's like behind closed doors. Amanda, however, she realized he was controlling, and Callan knows the truth about everything—everything except the baby inside me. My stomach lurches, and I swallow hard.

"Why don't we run out and get some food," I suggest. "I'm starving."

"I thought of that," he says and goes back outside.

I glance around for a phone, but no such luck, and mine is

still in his back pocket. He comes back in with two brown paper bags with food.

"I thought we'd cook together," he says. "Remember how we used to do that."

What I remember is him getting annoyed if I got in his way. "Yeah, big fun," I lie.

He removes the items from the bag and keeps casting glances my way. "What's the matter, Gemma?"

"Nothing," I say and try to hide my rising panic. "I just, yesterday I wasn't feeling well. I think my stomach is still upset." I jerk my thumb toward the bathroom. "Do you mind if I run in there for a bit."

He pulls a big knife from the drawer and I try not to react as he slices into an onion. "Yeah, don't be long."

"I'll just freshen up," I say and reach for my purse.

Before I can get away, he comes to me, opens my purse and looks into it. He pulls out my Tylenol bottle.

"What's this for."

"Like I said I wasn't feeling well yesterday and was a bit feverish. I'm going to take a couple of these."

He seems satisfied enough with the answer, and gives me my purse back. I hurry to the bathroom. I nearly cry out in relief when I see the window. It's small but I'm sure I can squeeze through it, and the baby isn't big enough for me to do any harm. I lock the door, turn on the water and tug on the window. Stupid thing is stuck. I tug some more, and it makes a loud cracking sound. I suck in a breath and go still.

"Gemma, what's going on in there?"

"I just dropped my medicine bottle. I'm going to gather the spilled pills. I'll be right out."

The door knob turns then stops. "Hurry it up." With my heart racing, I lift myself up, and slide out the small window. I land on the ground with a thud, pick myself up quickly and dash to the cabin, three doors down. I knock quietly and hug myself, expecting Brad to come rushing from the cottage. The door finally opens and a middle-aged man stands there.

"What can I do for you?"

I nearly cry with relief.

"What's going on, Dennis?" a woman calls out.

"Don't know," he says as I hurry inside and close and lock the door behind me.

I take a deep breath and blurt out, "Call 911."

18

CALLAN

"Now what?" I ask as Amanda stares at the laptop she's holding beside me.

"This exit right here," she says, and I flick on my signal.

I turn off the highway, and we come to a fork in the road. "That way," she says, checking Gemma's Find My Phone app on her laptop. For the first time, I'm glad she's always losing her phone, and installed the app on her devices.

"Where the fuck are we?" I ask, and work to fight down the rising panic.

Amanda glances around. "I don't know." Just then Amanda's phone rings and we exchange a worried glance. She checks it, and says, "It's Mom. What should I do?"

"You better answer it."

Amanda hesitates. "I don't want to worry her, though."

"But maybe she knows something. Maybe she's heard from her. You better answer. Put her on speakerphone."

"Okay," she says and slides her finger across the screen. "Hey Mom," she says in her best casual voice.

"Hey Amanda."

"What's up?"

"Have you been talking to Gemma?"

"Uh, yeah, I saw her today, actually." She fusses with the zipper on her purse, likely needing something to do with her hands. "We went shopping."

"Did you know she was back with Brad?"

My heart jumps. "Fuck," I murmur under my breath as I grip the steering wheel tighter.

"She never told me that, Mom."

"I thought it was strange, too. She seemed so happy with Callan. Happier than I've seen her in a long time. I was rooting for those two. I must say Misty and John are happy they're together again, though."

"When did you hear from her?" she asks.

"Oh, around dinner time. We were eating at the club when she called. Brad was with her."

"Did they say where they were going?"

"They were at her place, but Brad had something special planned for them." She stares at me, and her mom's voice pulls me back. "Amanda, is everything okay?"

"Yes, everything is fine," she says. "I'll talk to you soon."

"One more thing. She said she was going to call me when they reached their destination, but I haven't heard from her."

Amanda briefly closes her eyes to pull herself together. "I'm sure you'll hear from her soon enough."

"I'll let you know."

"Yes, please do. Love you, Mom."

"Love you too, dear."

She ends the call and when we come to a road that looks like it's lined with cottages, I slow to a stop and gesture to the computer. "Anything?"

She nods. "We should get out and walk."

"You're right."

We step from the car, and instantly hear pounding on a door.

"Callan," Amanda says her voice bordering on hysteria. "We have to do something."

"Get back in the car and call 911."

"I don't want to leave you out here. Brad's a cop. He has a gun."

"I know." I give her shoulders a squeeze and turn her to the car. My pulse is battering my throat as I walk toward the pounding noise and find Brad outside a cottage.

"Open up," he demands, his fist battering the door. "I just want to talk."

I exhale, and quickly figure out that Gemma is inside, and she must be safe.

"What's going on, Brad?" I ask and he spins so fast, he nearly falls off the top step.

"What the fuck are you doing here?" he asks.

"I could ask you the same question."

"Gemma and I are back together."

"Doesn't seem like that to me." Just then I catch sight of Gemma peeking out the window. I don't let on I see her, but I'm so goddamn happy she's okay, I can hardly breathe.

"We have some things to work out," Brad says.

I take a combative stance. "Why don't you work them out with me instead?"

He scoffs. "Get real, Callan. I'm a fucking cop."

"I don't care what you are. Come on down here," I say wanting to get him away from the door. He hesitates for a second. "Oh, I get it, you only like picking on people who can't fight back."

"Fuck off, Callan. This isn't your business."

"I love that woman in there and she's pregnant with my baby. So yeah, it's my fucking business."

"She's what?" he says through clenched teeth as I provoke his anger.

"You heard me."

"You're full of shit."

"Come find out."

With fight or flight kicking in, and I damn well plan to fight, adrenaline floods my body. Brad stomps down the steps and the second he's close enough, I hit him with every fucking ounce of anger in me, and he falters backward, dropping to his knees. Rage fuels me and I take a step toward him when the front door to the cottage opens, and in that split second of inattention, Brad goes for my legs, knocking me on my back. I go down with an oomph, and he climbs on top of me.

"You dumb fuck. Do you have any idea what's going to happen to you for hitting an officer?"

"Do you have any idea what's going to happen to you for kidnapping the woman I love?"

He pulls his arm back and I block his punch. I jerk him off me and we roll on the hard ground. As we struggle, he manages to pin me again, and I'm seconds from flipping him over when a crack reverberates in the air.

I look past his shoulders and find Gemma there, a big motherfucking tree branch in her hands. Brad slumps over me and as I push him off, sirens sound in the distance, and I'm not certain how they got here so fast.

Amanda comes running to us. "They were already on their way," she says and breaks into tears when she sees Gemma standing over me.

"Thanks, babe," I say, and Gemma laughs, an almost overwhelmed, hysterical laugh. She turns to hug her sister, and I jump to my feet and pull her to me when they break apart. "You're safe, Gemma. You're safe. I'm so fucking sorry this happened."

She pulls back and the strong woman that she is, she glares at me. "Don't for one minute blame yourself for this, Callan."

"I know. I won't."

"Good, because he was getting ready to break down that door and there could have been a very different outcome if you hadn't showed up." Police cars surround us, and an elderly man and woman come from the cottage and start giving all the details.

"We're going to need to take your statements," an officer says to Gemma as they cuff Brad and put him in the car.

"Can you give us a minute?" I ask. "She's been through a lot."

The officer nods and I step away with Gemma.

I pull her to me and kiss her head. "Gemma, my God. Are you okay?"

"Just shaken," she says, and hugs me so tight I can barely breathe.

"I was terrified," I admit. "Terrified something bad happened to you. I loved and lost once, and I was so scared it was going to happen again."

Her head lifts and she inches back. "Are you saying..."

"I'm saying I love you."

A sob catches in her throat. "Callan, I have to tell you something."

"Before you do, I need you to know that you never have to be afraid of me, afraid of telling me anything. I'd never hurt you."

"I know that. You're the best guy I know." She glances down. "But I'm..."

"Pregnant. I know."

Her head jerks up, her eyes wide.

"How...wait. Amanda, right?"

"Yeah, she had to tell me, and I'm so fucking sorry you

were afraid to tell me, afraid I'd be mad. I can understand where you were coming from, though, Gemma."

She blinks. "You can?"

"Of course. I said all along that I didn't want more, and it was true."

She sniffs. "Callan..."

"It *was* true, up until I met you." I sink to my knees, and put my arms around her, giving a gentle kiss to her stomach. "I want us to be together forever."

"Callan, no."

I look up at her. "What?"

"I don't want you saying these things because I'm pregnant. I know you'd never turn your back on our baby, but I don't have to come with the package. You don't have to do the noble thing."

"I love you, Gemma. I fucking love you. I want to be with you forever. I want us to raise this baby together, have more. Fill our house with kids. I want us to be a real family."

She drops to her knees in front of me, tears falling down her face. "I love you."

"Yeah?"

"Yeah," she says. I open my mouth and she puts her finger to it. "Don't ask me to marry you."

My heart falls into my stomach. "Gemma?"

She smiles. "Not here, not like this. My God, this is not the story I want to tell our kids."

Warmth and love move through me. "You're right. I'll make it special."

"Every day with you and Kaitlyn is special, Callan. I'm so crazy in love with you both."

I shake my head. "This is so not how I thought tonight was going to go down," I say.

"What do you mean?"

"If you have any doubts about my love, you won't once we get home."

"What did you do?"

"I had a special night planned, because I was going to spill my guts." I'm rewarded with a big laugh. "But it's all ruined."

"It doesn't have to be ruined," she says. "Let's give our statements, call my parents, and then call Kaitlyn, tell them all the good news."

"I'd love that."

"Then we can go home, and you can show me just how much you love me."

I put my hand on her cheek. "I like the way you think."

She puts her hand on my cheek, her eyes slowly moving over my face, a careful assessment. "You good, Callan?"

"I'm good, Gemma," I say and this time I really and truly mean it and she really and truly knows it. "I'm really good, thanks to you."

"Right back at ya, Callan."

"Good, now come on. Let's go get the rest of our lives started."

***

Thank you so much for reading, **Single Dad Burning. Keep an eye out for Single Dad with Benefits. Please read on for** an excerpt of **The Playmaker,** book one in my **Players on Ice Series.**

The Playmaker

NINA:

Fat drops of spring rain pummel my head, wilting my curls as I dart through Seattle's busy traffic to the café on the other side of the street. My best friend, Jess, is inside waiting for me, undoubtedly hyped up on her third latté by now.

I step over a pothole and search for an opening in the traffic. I hate being late, I really do. I totally value other people's time, but when the email came through from my editor, asking me to write a hot hockey series, my priorities took a curve. I've worked with Tara for a couple years now, and I know her like—pardon the pun—a well-worn book. To her, hesitation equals disinterest. She's a mover, a tree-shaker, and it wouldn't have taken long for her to offer the opportunity to another author. She wanted a quick reply and I had to give it to her.

I got this!

Yeah, that was my response, but what did I have to lose? I've been in such a rut lately, thanks to my fickle muse, deserting me when I needed her most. I swear to God, sometimes she acts like a hormonal teenager. I need to whip her into shape so I don't lose this gig. The royalties from a series will help make a sizeable dent in the bills that are piling up high and deep.

High and deep.

I laugh. One of those self-derisive snorts that crawls out when you'd really rather cry. Yeah, that pretty much sums up the *I got this* response I emailed back. High and deep, like a big steaming pile of—

A car horn blares, jolting me from my pity party. With my heart pounding in my chest, I step in front of the Tesla and flip the guy off. I safely reach the sidewalk and once again my mind is back on my job, and off the impatient jerk in the overpriced car.

I step up on the sidewalk and lift my face to the rain, the cool water a pleasant break from this unusual spring heat wave we're having. Pressure fills my throat. The hum of traffic behind me dulls, leaving only the sound of my pulse pounding in my ears. Panic.

Why the hell did my editor think I, former figure skater turned romance novelist, would want to write a series about hot hockey players? Yeah, sure my brother is an NHL player, but that doesn't mean I'm into the game. I hate hockey. No, hate is too mild a word for what I feel. I loathe it entirely. But you know what I don't loathe? Eating. Yeah, I like eating. Oh, and a roof over my head. I really like that, too.

I draw in a semi self-satisfied breath at having rationalized my fast response.

Except my reply was total and utter bullshit. I don't *got this*. In fact, I...wait, what's the antonym of *got this*? All that comes to mind is, *you're screwed*. Yep, that pretty much describes my predicament.

Why didn't I just stick to figure skating?

Because you took a bad spill that ended your career.

Oh right. But seriously, a hockey series... Ugh. Kill me. Freaking. Now.

I reach the café, pull the glass door open and slick my rain-soaked hair from my face. I quickly catalogue the place to find Jess hitting on the barista. Ahh, now I get why she picked a place so far from home. I take in the guy behind the counter. Damn, he's hotter than the steaming latté in Jess's hand, and from the way she's flirting, it's clear he'll be in her bed later today.

I sigh inwardly. It's always so easy for her. Me? Not so much. Men rarely pay me attention. Unlike Jess, I'm plain, have the body of a twelve-year-old boy, and most times I blend into the woodwork.

I pick up a napkin from the side counter and mop the rain off my face. Doesn't matter. I'm not interested anyway. From my puck-bunny-chasing brother to all his cocky friends, I know what guys are really like, and when it comes to women, they're only after one thing, and it isn't scoring the slot. I roll my eyes. Then again, maybe it is.

And of course, I can't forget the last guy I was set up with. What he did to me was totally abusive, but I don't want to dredge up those painful memories right now.

I shake, and water beads fall right off my brand-new rain-resistance coat. At least something is going right for me today. Semi-dry, I cross the room and stand beside Jess.

"Hey, sorry I'm late."

Jess turns to me, smiles, and holds a finger up. "I'll forgive you only if you're late because you were knees deep into some nasty sex, 'cause girlfriend, it's been far too long since you've been laid."

Jesus, what ever happened to this girl's filters?

Thoroughly embarrassed, my gaze darts to the barista, who is grinning, his eyes still locked on my friend, looking at her like she's today's hot lunch special and ignoring me like I'm yesterday's cold, lumpy oatmeal.

Ugh, really?

"Non-fat latté," I say, and scowl at him until he puts his eyes back in his head. I might be an English major but I have a PhD in the death glare. Truthfully, I'm so sick of guys like him, one thing on their minds. Then again, Jess only wants one thing from him, so I really shouldn't have a problem with it. Why do I? Oh, maybe because Mr. Right, my battery-operated companion, isn't quite cutting it anymore, and it's left me a little jittery and a whole lot cranky.

Jess is right. I *do* need to get laid.

Jess's lips flatline when she takes me in, her gaze carefully accessing me. "What?" she asks, her mocha eyes narrowing.

God, sometimes I really hate how well she can read me. "Nothing."

She straightens to her full height, and I try to do the same, but she dwarfs me, even without her beloved two-inch heels. I square my shoulders, but it's always hard to pull off a high-power pose when you're only five foot two, and teased relentlessly about it.

"Come on," she says, and guides me to a corner table. I peel off my coat and plunk down. Jess sits across from me. "Spill."

I point to my forehead. "Do I have 'idiot' written here?"

She looks me over, and cautiously asks, "No, why?"

My phone chirps in my purse, and I reach for it. Great, it's my editor wanting to set turn-in dates. "How about never?" I say under my breath.

"Uh, Nina. You're talking to your phone. You better tell me what's going on."

"You're not going to believe what I just agreed to."

"Do tell," she says and leans forward, like I'm about to spill some dirty little sex secret. If only that were the case.

I grab my phone and hold it up, showing her Tara's message. "I just agreed to write a hockey series," I say, and toss my phone back into my purse, mic-drop style—without the bold confidence.

Jess pushes back in her chair, clearly disappointed. She lifts her cup, and over the rim, asks, "I don't see how that makes you an idiot."

My mouth drops open. Jess and I have been friends since childhood. She of all people knows how much I hate hockey. "Are you serious?"

She shrugs. "You're a writer."

Mr. Sexy Barista brings me my coffee and he shares a secret, let's-hook-up-later smile with Jess. "And...?" I ask when he leaves.

"Writer's write and make things up. I know you hate hockey, but what does that have to do with anything?"

"I can't come up with a plot, or write about the game, if I don't know anything about it."

She shakes her head. "And I can't believe your brother is a professional player and you never once paid attention to the game."

"I was busy pursuing a professional skating career, remember?"

She reaches across the table and gives my hand a little squeeze. "I know. I'm sorry."

My tailbone and neck take that moment to throb, a constant reminder of a career lost.

I didn't just lose my dream of skating professionally the day my feet went out from underneath me, I lost my confidence, too. A concussion will do that to you.

Good thing I majored in English in college. Once I hung up my skates, I began to blog about the sport and sold a few articles. I joined a local writers group, and after talking to a group of romance writers, I tried my hand at one. Much to my surprise, it actually sold. I went from non-fiction to fiction, in every sense of the word. Happily ever after might exist between the pages, but it certainly doesn't in real life. At least not for me.

I take a sip of my latté, and give an exaggerated huff as I set it down. Jess instantly goes into problem-solving mode when she sees that I'm really stressed about this. As a brand-new high school guidance counselor, she can't help but want to fix me.

"Okay, it's simple," she begins. "You have to learn the game."

"How am I supposed to do that?"

"Turn on the TV and watch."

"I can watch a bunch of guys chase a stupid puck around a rink all I want, I still won't be able to understand the rules."

"How dare you call my favorite sport stupid."

"Jessss..." I plead. "What am I going to do?"

She crinkles her nose. Then her eyes go wide. "I've got it. Shadow your brother."

I give a quick shake of my head. "No, he's on the road, and he won't want me hanging around."

Jess goes quiet again, and that hollowed-out spot inside me aches as I think about Cason. I miss my brother so much and wish we were closer. Cason and I grew up in a family where there were no hugs or words of affirmation. I know Mom and Dad loved us, but as busy investment bankers, work consumed their lives. Sure, they put me in figure skating, and Cason in hockey when we were young, but they never shared in our passions, or really supported our pursuits.

I guess I can't expect my brother to display love, when none was ever displayed to him.

"Why don't you teach me?"

"It might be my favorite sport to watch, but I don't really know all the rules. I think you'd be better off getting your brother or..." She straightens. "Wait. I got this," she says, and I cringe when she tosses my three-word email response back at me. A warning shiver skips along my spine, and I get the sense that whatever she's about suggest, is going to take me right down the rabbit hole.

"What about Cole Cannon?"

I groan, plant my elbows on the table, and cover my face with my hands. "Never," I mumble through my fingers. "Not in a million freaking years."

Jess removes my hands from my face. "Why not? He's your brother's best friend. I'm sure he'll help you."

"Cocky Cole Cannon, aka, The Playmaker. Do I need to say any more?" I reach for my latté and take a huge gulp, burning the roof of my mouth. Damn.

"I know you hate him, Nina, but—"

"Of course I hate him. You remember the nickname he used to use when we were kids—Pretty BallerNina. I was a figure skater, not a ballerina," I could only assume he was mocking me about being pretty too, but I keep that to myself.

"At least he worked your name into the moniker, and hey, it could have been worse. He could have called you Neaner Neaner, like Cason did."

I glare at her and she holds her hands up. "Okay, okay. I get it. But Cole's been home for a month, recovering from a concussion, and his team—the Seattle Shooters, in case you don't know the league's name," she adds with a wink, "are probably going to make it to the playoffs, so you know he's watching all the games. You don't have to like him to ask him to explain a few of the plays, right?"

"I suppose."

Wait! What? Am I really thinking about asking The Playmaker to help me? I reach for my latté and blow on it before I take another big gulp.

"And if you ask me, while he's helping you learn the plays, I think you two should hate fuck."

I choke on my drink, spitting most of it on my friend as the rest dribbles down my chin.

OMFG, how embarrassing. All eyes turn to me. Mortified, I grab a napkin and start wiping my face, but Jess is laughing so hard, I start laughing with her.

"Couldn't you have waited until I swallowed?" I ask.

"That's what she said."

"Ohmigod, Jess. How are we friends?"

She waves a dismissive hand. "You know you love me because I'm hellacioulsy funny."

"I do, just stop cracking jokes when I'm drinking."

She leans towards me conspiratorially, and I brace myself. "I wasn't joking. You and Cocky Cole Cannon should hate fuck. He's as sexy today as he was when he used to hang out with Cason at your house when we were teens." I give her a look that suggests she's insane. She ignores it and wags her brows. "He's explosive on the ice, but do you know why they really call him the Cannon?"

"Because it's his last name."

"Yeah, but that's not the only reason."

Don't ask. Don't ask.

"Okay, then why?" I ask.

"'Cause he's loaded between his legs."

Yeah, okay, I totally set myself up for that.

"You don't know that," I shoot back. My mind races to my brother's best friend, and I mentally go over his form. He's athletic, tall and—as much as I hate to admit it—hot as hell. The perfect trifecta. Could he be packing too? Working with some top-notch equipment?

Jesus, what am I doing? The last thing I should be thinking about is Cole's 'cannon'.

"Come on." Jess grabs her purse. "I'll drive you there."

I flatten my hands on the table. "I'm not going to his house, especially not unannounced."

"Give him a call then."

"No."

She sits back in her chair and folds her arms, a sign she's changing tactics. "And here I thought you liked your condo and food in your cupboards."

I groan at the direct hit.

Her voice softens and she touches my hand. "But you know you always have—"

"Fine." I stop her before she brings up my trust fund. Yeah, sure, Mom and Dad set money aside for me, but I don't want to use it. I want to live by my own means, make it on my own merit. Besides it wasn't their money I wanted, then or now, it was their attention, their love. I moved out years ago and only ever hear from them on my birthday or at Christmas.

I pull my phone from my purse. "I'll text him. If he doesn't answer, we don't talk about this again." I go through my contacts and find his number, having stored it years ago when he called to check on me after my injury. The call had taken me by surprise; so did his concern. Maybe my brother put him up to it. I don't know. Nor do I know why I kept his number.

My fingers fly across the screen, but in no way do I expect him to respond. At least I hope he doesn't. I read over the text. *Sorry to hear about your concussion. I was wondering if you could help me with something.* Then hit send.

I set my phone down and look at Jess. "Happy?"

"Hey, I'm not the one who's going to be homeless."

Point taken. Maybe I should be hoping he *does* text back.

My phone pings, and we both reach for it. Jess gets it first, and from her smirk, I guess my wish just came true—Colin responded.

Careful what you wish for.

"What does it say?" I ask, afraid of the answer.

"It says, sure what's up?" Jess's fingers dance over the screen as she responds for me.

"What are you saying?" I ask, panic welling up inside me. "So help me, if you're telling him I need to get laid..."

The phone pings again and she holds it out for me to read.

"I asked—I mean *you* asked if you could stop by his place, and he said sure."

"I don't know whether to kiss you or choke you," I say.

Jess laughs. "I think you'll be thanking me." She stands. "Come on."

We make our way outside, and the rain has slowed to a light mist as I follow her down the street to her parked car. I hop in and question my sanity. Am I really going to ask Cocky Cannon to teach me the game?

Jess starts the car and the locks click as she pulls into traffic. Guess so.

"You remember where he lives?" I ask. I think back to when he bought the house. He had a big party to celebrate. I was invited but didn't go. Why would I? Watching the hockey players with their bunnies was not my idea of a good time.

"Of course." She jacks the tunes and sings along off-key as she drives. Twenty minutes later, she pulls up in front of his mansion. It's a ridiculously big house for one person. I stare at it, and once again question my sanity.

"Go," Jess says.

"I'm going," I shoot back. I open the door, and smooth my hand over my mess of curls. Why the hell did I do that? It's not like I'm trying to make myself presentable or impress him. We don't even like each other.

I force my legs to carry me to his door, and I'm about to knock when it opens. My breath catches as I take in Cole, standing before me shirtless and barefoot, dressed only in a pair of faded jeans that hug him so nicely.

God, he is so freaking hot—and I never, ever should have come here.

As we stare at each other, like we're in some goddamn Mexican standoff, I can't stop thinking about his 'cannon'. My gaze drops to the lovely bulge between his legs, and a moan I have no control over catches in my throat as Jess's words come back to haunt me.

You two should hate fuck.

Thank you, Jess, for planting that idea in my brain. Christ, I should have choked her when I had the chance.

***

If you want to find out what kind of trouble Nina and Cole get into check it out here: **The Playmaker**

ALSO BY CATHRYN FOX

Big Catch

Brazilian Fantasy

Improper Proposal

Boys of Beachville

Good at Being Bad

Igniting the Bad Boy

Bad Girl Therapy

Stone Cliff Series:

Crashing Down

Wasted Summer

Love Lessons

Wrapped Up

Eternal Pleasure Series

Instinctive

Impulsive

Indulgent

Sun Stroked Series

Seaside Seduction

Deep Desire

Private Pleasure

Captured and Claimed Series:

Yours to Take

Yours to Teach

Yours to Keep

Firefighter Heat Series

Fever

Siren

Flash Fire

Playing For Keeps Series

Slow Ride

Wild Ride

Sweet Ride

Breaking the Rules:

Hold Me Down Hard

Pin Me Up Proper

Tie Me Down Tight

Stand Alone Title:

Hands on with the CEO

Torn Between Two Brothers

Holiday Spirit

Unleashed

Knocking on Demon's Door

Web of Desire

ABOUT CATHRYN

New York Times and *USA today* Bestselling author, Cathryn is a wife, mom, sister, daughter, and friend. She loves dogs, sunny weather, anything chocolate (she never says no to a brownie) pizza and red wine. She has two teenagers who keep her busy with their never ending activities, and a husband who is convinced he can turn her into a mixed martial arts fan. Cathryn can never find balance in her life, is always trying to find time to go to the gym, can never keep up with emails, Facebook or Twitter and tries to write page-turning books that her readers will love.

Connect with Cathryn:
Newsletter https://app.mailerlite.com/webforms/landing/c1f8n1
Twitter: https://twitter.com/writercatfox
Facebook: https://www.facebook.com/AuthorCathrynFox?ref=hl
Blog: http://cathrynfox.com/blog/
Goodreads: https://www.goodreads.com/author/show/91799.Cathryn_Fox

Pinterest http://www.pinterest.com/catkalen/